THE VAMPIRE'S FAMILIAR

FAMILIAR MATES

TJ NICHOLS

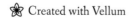

Thank you for buying The Vampire's Familiar. Get a free copy of A Wolf's Resistance when you join my newsletter. http://www.tjnichols-author.com/lp/

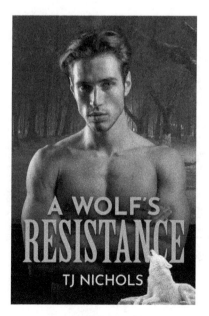

A gay shifter novella

THE VAMPIRE'S FAMILIAR

He came looking for revenge. Will he walk away from love?

Twenty years after fleeing Madison Gully as a scared sixteen-year-old, after witnessing his sister's murder, Kirk Gracewell returns as a powerful energy vampire. He wants to find the cougar shifter who killed her and make them pay.

Every ten years, the Madison cougars get together. It's a time of celebration to meet new partners but also for the seer announce who'll get the greatest honor any of them can receive: becoming a familiar to a witch.

When the seer gives Sage the task of watching the vampire that's suddenly arrived, Sage feels slighted; it's a job for a much younger cougar. But he comes to enjoy the games of cat and mouse he plays with Kirk. Until he learns why the vampire is in Madison Gully. Now Sage will have to choose: protect his family or help Kirk find the killer.

But the killer will stop at nothing to prove to the seer the honor of familiar is his, claim a witch, and bury the past.

CHAPTER ONE

THE NEED TO return home had been gnawing in Kirk Gracewell's blood for the better part of a month. Not that Madison Gully had been his home in a very long time. Now as he stood watching the sunrise crest the hills behind Madison Ranch, while the town slept in the shadows, he wasn't sure why he'd waited so long.

Twenty years since he'd fled. It had been ten years since he'd dreamed of Abby, but last night she'd haunted his dreams. The scar on his palm had been itching, reminding him of the rash promise he'd made to his sister.

The papers had said suicide, but that was bullshit. He'd watched the cougar attack Abby in the middle of town, and the only cougars in Madison Gully were the Madisons.

He'd sworn revenge and had let it go cold. Now Abby was pulling him home.

He cracked his knuckles and leaned against his motorbike as he waited for sunlight to tip over the hill and illuminate the valley. The air was still full of winter cold and sharp where the city air was a dull knife. From his vantage point Madison Gully was still the same. The only thing that had changed was him. A few more minutes wouldn't matter. He'd get breakfast and coffee in the diner which probably hadn't changed one bit.

Liquid gold finally spilled over the hills and the town that had grown up around the ranch over a century ago. He held his breath hoping for some kind of joy at returning. Nothing. Not a damn thing. This trip raised nothing more than the average emotion that came with running an errand—something akin to annoyance at having to go out of his way.

When he'd left, the anger and fear and shame had burned with every breath.

He'd half expected to be killed, or blamed.

Mom had been blamed for Dad's death. She'd even blamed herself. And then she'd killed herself. For a year it had been just him and Abby, scraping by as best they could.

And he'd failed her when she'd needed him.

For a heartbeat despair tried to drag him down. But he had to be here. That need was like a drum in his chest getting louder the longer he waited. He'd tried to turn his vintage bike around several times, yet every time the need in his blood became more insistent. Abby needed justice, and she'd waited long enough.

Maybe after this he'd be able to move on with his life.

He closed his eyes and drew in a breath, tasting the life and feeling it vibrate against his skin. That was all he wanted. To be free. After everything was that too much to ask?

He opened his eyes, to see the town now bathed in sunlight.

Kirk smiled, cracked his knuckles again, and then pulled on his gloves ready to hunt cougar. He'd be gone again in less than a week and no one would know it was him. There was nothing in Madison Gully that could make him stay.

———

MADISON RANCH WAS CLOSED to visitors for two weeks. That meant no dealing with wannabe cowboys who knew nothing about anything with four legs. Most couldn't light a fire without burning their eyebrows off. The break should have been something close to a holiday for Sage Madison, but his family had already started arriving.

By family he meant everyone from cousins to cousins twice removed and their newest baby. Half of them he didn't know and couldn't have picked out in a line up if his life depended on it. The only thing he knew was that they all smelled like shifters, even the human partners.

Honestly, he didn't like so many people around.

He sat with his bacon and eggs near the alpaca pen and enjoyed the relative silence with black coffee and a headache at the base of his skull from drinking a bit too much bourbon last night with the cousins he did know. He was the baby of the group even though he was thirty. As he shoveled in the last hash brown, he hoped their age was against them and their hangovers laid them low all day. He smiled and drank his coffee, happy with the sun on his face.

He closed his eyes, tipped his head back against the fence post, and ran through the list of things he needed to do around the ranch. Just because there were no paying holiday makers didn't mean there wasn't things to do. The animals all had to be fed, there was a fence that needed a little work before it came down in the next storm, and the usual assortment of other tasks that filled his days.

Given the hangovers going around he doubted he'd get much help. Which was fine, as it would give him an excuse to get away from everyone and the not so subtle questions about why he was still single.

Soft footsteps came toward him, and he hoped they'd keep walking by. They didn't of course. He knew before he opened his eyes who it was. She smelled like her name, Violet, though he'd heard a rumor that in her younger years she'd been nicknamed 'Violent' for the constant scraps she got into. Not that he'd risk making a reference to them.

Sage squinted into the sunlight that haloed the seer's white-blond hair. "Were you looking for me?"

Of course she was; Violet didn't wander around aimlessly. With everyone gathered here, she was busy either talking or meditating to get her predictions right. While she only lived three hours away Sage hadn't seen her in four years. That had been her fiftieth.

She studied him for a moment and nodded, more to herself than him.

Most people would want her to read their futures so they could be aware of any upcoming obstacles. He'd avoided doing that at the last gathering ten years ago and had planned to do much the same this time. He was happy with the way things were and didn't want to risk hearing something that he didn't like the sound of.

What if she told him he needed to leave the ranch to find a partner?

Or that the ranch should've gone to his uncle? His uncle had expected to inherit the ranch on his brother's death, but it had been left to Mom. That had been the start of the bitterness. Eventually his uncle had demanded to be paid out his share, hoping to force her to sell so no one got the ranch. But Mom was smart. She'd been ready for trouble and had given him the money. Him and his boys left Madison Gully. Now they only came back for gatherings, sneering, and sniping.

Last night the cousins had all placed bets on who would be the next familiar, and Sage joined in. His name had come up, but had been quickly scrubbed out, everyone knowing why without it being said, but it still hurt. He knew the honor of being a witch's mate wasn't for him. He wasn't a Madison by blood.

Sage lifted his eyebrows but didn't try to hurry Violet along. He had a few minutes to spare before he had to get moving. The first job he did would be to swallow some aspirin and drink some water. The coffee didn't seem to be helping much, or maybe it was the sun in his eyes, but for a moment he was so dizzy he was sure he was about to fall over. He reached a hand back to grab the fence, closed his eyes, and immediately felt better.

"I need you to do something for me, Sage." Violet's voice was close and when he opened his eyes, she was squatting in front of him like they were trading secrets.

"Sure." Because saying no and getting on her bad side wasn't on his to do list.

"But I don't want anyone else to know."

"Um...okay." He sat up straight and ignored the throb in his temple like a horse had kicked him in the head. The bacon and eggs swam greasily in his stomach; they might have been a bad idea. "What?"

Was she planning a secret baby shower for someone who didn't even know yet? Or did she just want him to pick up her favorite chocolate and vodka and she didn't want to share? She could've asked anyone, but she'd searched him out.

He swallowed and wished he wasn't feeling like yesterday's leftovers.

"There's a vampire in town."

Sage tilted his head and stared at her as if her words would suddenly make sense. "A vampire? Aren't they meant to be extinct?"

"That's what they wanted the world to believe." She shrugged like it didn't matter. "I want you to keep an eye on him."

"What does he look like?"

"No idea, I just felt his arrival." She fluttered her fingers. "Like a fly on my web."

How did he put this politely? "I've got ranch business to take care of."

He didn't have time to keep an eye on a not quite extinct paranormal that Violet had sensed, but never seen.

"Your cousins can pull their weight and get their hands dirty."

Sage groaned. "They don't know what they're doing. I should stay and—"

"*You* need to follow the vampire." The way she said told Sage it there would be no further argument.

He wasn't a cub who needed a mission to give him something to do; that happened plenty to keep them out of trouble. He didn't want to be chasing after should-be-dead vampires. He'd much rather be mucking out the stables. He could think of about a hundred things he'd rather do than go into town. "Everyone is here."

"All the more reason for you to go."

"But..." There were no buts. Her face was impassive. He was being sent away from the ranch during the gathering. His heart sank. Was his dubious blood line finally catching up with him? "Am I in trouble?"

"No." She clasped a strong hand around his upper arm. "Only you can do this for me. It's not something I hand over lightly. I've been dwelling on it since sunup, but I can't ignore the signs."

"Am I banished to town?"

Violet shook her head. "I need you to find out his name. Get me something of his so I can see him. But don't tell anyone what you're doing for me."

"Then what do I say? Stone and the others will whine

about doing my chores." His brothers and cousins tended to treat this as a holiday, not realizing the extra work they made.

"They can bitch to me. All they need to know is that I've sent you on errands." She stood and stretched.

His brother and older cousins wouldn't complain to her, but they would see him as little more than a cub, doing the bidding of the elders. Even though the seer was asking him to do this for her, Sage still couldn't shake off the feeling that he was being demoted to a much lesser position in the family hierarchy.

He worked his tail off for his family and the ranch and it still wasn't enough. Maybe he should've gotten a fancy degree and left like the others, but he'd never wanted to leave the ranch.

Violet offered him a hand up and he accepted. To do otherwise would be churlish and he didn't want to slide any further until it was easy to kick him out. Maybe this was some kind of test.

She put her hand over his and breathed, "Thank you. This is important. I can feel it."

Sage wanted to believe her, but it still felt like a waste of his time. He'd run the vampire off and then get back to avoiding his extended family.

CHAPTER TWO

THE DINER WAS NO LONGER the only place to grab a cheap bite in town, but it was familiar and his first choice. Kirk parked his bike out the front and sat for a moment before pulling off his helmet. If he ignored the newer model cars, and the new cupcake cafe up the road just next to the bar that now doubled as a burger serving family restaurant, Madison Gully was the same.

The video shop where Abby had worked had been replaced by cupcakes.

The bloodstain out back would also be gone.

For a moment the memories were too much. He knew every street pole he'd been shoved into by the older Madisons. He flexed his fingers then drew off his gloves. He needed to eat before he went to the cemetery. Hopefully the diner still served Abby's favorite cherry pie. He'd get a piece for her; after so many years it was the least he could do.

While he knew ghosts didn't exist, there were other things to be afraid of. He was one of the things people liked to pretend didn't exist.

He swung his leg over the bike, shoved his gloves in his

pocket and, keeping his helmet under his arm, went in. The bell chimed and two of the people already seated looked over. The rest all had headphones in and were staring at their laptops or tablets.

Kirk didn't recognize anyone. A little of the tension that had been wrapped around his chest like barbed wire slipped free and he took a seat in a booth with his back to the kitchen so he could face the door. Too many nights of sleeping rough in the city had made him careful of his surroundings. Too many years living with his now dead mentor had cured him of trusting anyone.

A dark-haired woman approached him with a worn-out smile. It wasn't even nine and she looked done for the day. "What can I get you?"

"Coffee." He hadn't even had time to check the menu, and he didn't really care. He'd manage a few bites, but too much food didn't agree with him. She might make a nice snack, though. "Pancakes with extra syrup." He gave her a grin. "*Real* maple syrup."

She didn't return his smile. "Sure. Small or large stack."

"Small." And it had better be real syrup. Real syrup had energy vibrations that fake couldn't match. And while he didn't get much nourishment from food, he took what he could.

"That all?"

"For the moment."

She cast her gaze over him again and he wondered if he'd gone to school with her. The high school was in the next town. Most of them had caught the bus, the Madisons had been driven. "If you're looking for somewhere to stay, the ranch is closed for the next two weeks. Some family thing."

He hadn't planned on staying there—that would've been a little obvious. But he'd called and tried to book, only to be told it was closed for two weeks, confirming that the whole family would be there, just like when Abby was killed.

"So, I heard. I've booked a room at the B&B." He knew the house. It had once belonged to his favorite primary school teacher. Now it was four rooms decked out in blue and white check. Cute if you liked that kind of thing. It was too much like the home he'd always wanted but never had.

The pulse in his gut, the need that had driven him here hadn't abated. Gut instinct was one thing that his mentor had been very clear on; it was never wrong. People came unstuck when they stopped listening. And most people stopped listening because they didn't like what was being said. Ten years ago, he hadn't been strong enough to take on a cougar. He flexed his fingers. Now he was.

"So, what brings you here?"

"Family."

With the whole clan here, he could take them all out. No... that would make him no better than his mentor. All he wanted was Abby's killer brought to justice. Real justice, not the paltry three months behind bars the killer would get when his behavior was excused because of his good name or some lie that Abby had once smiled at him or said hello. No, Kirk would kill the cougar and make sure the cougar knew why.

The waitress considered him again. All he wanted her to do was get his damn coffee. Her gaze dropped to his hands. No rings. Scars on his knuckles like he'd been in one too many bar fights. Only a witch in the know, or another vampire, would understand what the scars were.

They weren't random at second glance. Or even pretty patterns. They were part of the spell that made him. He automatically laced his fingers, hiding them as much as he could.

"Enjoy your stay."

He was sure he wouldn't. Death was a hollow meal.

As she walked to the kitchen to hand over his order, he knew that in under three minutes the entire town would know there was fresh meat, single and eating pancakes alone. Gossip cast a wide spell no matter where it travelled. Tongues must be already flapping with all the Madisons in town. Now him.

He was fairly sure the Gracewells didn't rate too highly anymore on the gossip scale. The school cleaner who'd killed herself and left two kids behind had been a sad story that people had moved on from pretty fast. The offered help had vanished before the flowers on his mother's grave had wilted.

Abby had dropped out of school and gone full time at the video store. He'd been a little shit and picked fights with everyone more often suspended than at school. Happy times.

He cracked his knuckles, his stomach torn between hunger and the need to do something now he was here. What, he didn't know.

If his gut would engage his brain, he might be able to work out the compulsion and make a plan besides sneaking onto the ranch and finding the shifter responsible.

Abby's killer was an out of towner—thus why it had happened when the Madison's gathered. Everyone knew they did it every ten years. How many cougars were on the ranch, he didn't know, but he could eliminate anyone under the age of about thirty-three. Shifters only started shifting when puberty hit. And it had been a man.

His coffee arrived and he made the unnecessary but deliberate move of taking the cup from the waitress. Their skin touched and her energy, her life, flowed into him. She tasted like pie crust. Flaky, sweet and buttery. Delicious.

She blinked and almost dropped the pot of coffee. Some sloshed on the table. "Sorry."

He grabbed some napkins and cleaned up the spill, it was

his fault anyway. "No trouble. Maybe you need to sit down and have a cup."

Her face hardened like he'd suggested she join him. He hadn't been flirting with her. She needed juice and a cookie, much like after giving blood. What he'd done was certainly no more harmful. She'd be fine.

"I'll bring your stack when it's ready." She spun in her white sneakers and strode away.

Kirk shook his head and poured sugar into the cup. He licked his lower lip. So far breakfast wasn't too bad. He sniffed the coffee; it didn't have that burned left-too-long-in-the-pot scent that many had. Most people didn't notice those small things, like the way energy moved around and between people and things. Burnt coffee had nothing good left for anyone.

He leaned back in the seat content to sip coffee and watch the other diners, and the people on the street. He'd stood on the other side of the door too often counting the loose change in his pocket, knowing that if he bought a milkshake instead of bread there'd be nothing for lunch for the rest of the week. If he'd had this magic back then, he wouldn't have gone hungry so often.

The waitress's footsteps moved toward him. He closed his eyes and cradled the coffee like it was all he needed in the world. He couldn't be bothered making more polite conversation. The plate tapped the table and the scent of the hot syrup wafted toward him.

"Enjoy your breakfast." She didn't bother faking sincerity.

"Thanks." He opened his eyes but didn't look at her. Instead he dipped his finger in the syrup and tasted it. Fake syrup was useless to him. The sweetness settled on his tongue with the tiniest of tremors. He nodded.

She didn't care. She was already walking away.

The pancakes were exactly as he'd expected, thick, fluffy, and drowning in butter and syrup. He picked up his fork and broke off a mouthful of sodden bottom pancake—the best bit, and given that he'd only eat about a quarter of what was on his plate he wasn't going to waste time with un-drenched pancakes. He savored that first bite, the way it melted on his tongue and the sweetness that bloomed in his mouth. Even if he enjoyed the rest of his meal, nothing would be as good as that first bite.

It had taken him along time to appreciate the magic of the first bite and the way it felt on his tongue. But as he was able to eat less and less food, eating had become more about quality than quantity. Twenty years ago, he wouldn't have even understood the concept of quality. He just wanted food and as much as he could get as there was never enough.

The door chimed and a blond man in jeans and a dark blue jacket walked in. He nodded to a couple at the table on the other side of the diner and made his way over to the counter. Kirk watched the way the man walked and appreciated the way his thighs filled his jeans before the little scratch in his mind became more of a warning.

The man walked *too* smoothly, and he was *too* self-assured.

A Madison cougar.

And just like that, Kirk's breakfast was ruined. He didn't even need to feel the energy vibration to confirm the man was a shifter.

The man chatted to the waitress who laughed like they were old friends; they probably were. This was the kind of town where everyone knew each other. But if any humans knew the Madison family secret, it had certainly never gone public. Not even in this age of instant celebrity and social media.

Even though he knew the town needed the business of the ranch, he hadn't expected everyone to agree that Abby's murder was a suicide. If he hadn't been running late because he'd been playing video games at a friend's place...

He stabbed the pancake, knowing full well that if he'd met his sister as planned, they'd probably both be dead. There'd been a time when he believed that might've been for the best. He moved the drier bits to the side of the plate so he could make the most of the good bits. Yeah, he played with his food, but he didn't care what people thought. If they bitched, they'd be his next meal.

It took everything he had not to look up as the man walked over. There were plenty of free tables; why did he want a booth near him?

Or was Kirk sitting in the man's favorite seat?

But the man didn't take a different booth. He slid in opposite Kirk like they knew each other.

Neither of them said anything. It was that moment of assessing, when they each knew the other wasn't as human as they looked but neither wanted to admit what they were with humans around. Some things weren't discussed where people could hear.

The man's pale blond hair was slicked back. His blue eyes had that summer sky quality, that made them seem to go on forever. On another man, he might have found them pretty. He also lacked the pointed cat jaw line that many of the Madison's had. Pity their blood ran in his veins.

The Madison's gaze slid over him, no doubt taking in the black leather jacket, well creased with use, hair that was cut too short to be fashionable, and eyes that were no longer truly brown but something closer to amber. They'd get redder as he got older. His mentor had taken to wearing tinted glasses all the time to avoid the stares.

Even if the Madison knew Kirk wasn't human, he probably didn't know what he was. Most didn't and were too polite to ask. Kirk didn't enlighten them. His mentor had warned him that vampires would be hunted down by the Coven, the governing body of all paranormals, if they were discovered.

Kirk ate another bite of pancake and didn't taste a thing.

The man sipped his takeaway coffee. He hadn't planned on staying in the diner, so why had he decided to join him? Kirk was tempted to ask, but he didn't want to break the silence. Three more bites, then he was walking out and leaving some bills on the table.

He ate another mouthful, trying to work out which Madison this was. They all had stupid names. He'd been in the same class as Stone. Smart and popular and didn't he know it. A few years above him had been two others. Zinc? Copper? And Ash. He remembered Ash with his glacial eyes and cruel humor.

But this man was younger. The Madison glanced at the paper cup, took a sip, and then tilted his head as though looking at something just out of focus.

Kirk could practically see the Madison's whiskers twitching.

"So you're..." Madison lifted his eyebrows like he expected Kirk to fill in the blank.

"Eating breakfast." He took his second to last bite.

Madison smiled. "Want to tell me why you're here?"

"No. I don't need permission." To be in the town or enter a home; that was all stupid superstition. Crucifixes had no effect either. He wasn't dead. He didn't even drink blood. Though he could draw energy from freshly spilled blood, a talent that had probably contributed to the vampire myth.

"Got a name?"

"Yep. You?"

Madison almost laughed, then his smile fell away and he whispered, "I didn't think your kind existed anymore."

Kirk kept his features carefully schooled. This man knew what he was; that wasn't a good thing. "Officially we don't."

The Coven didn't like to admit vampires were real. It was magic they'd tried to eradicate about two hundred years ago, forcing those who remained underground—in some cases literally.

Kirk ate his last bite of pancake and finished his coffee. "You've had your three questions, so here are mine. Why did you come over? And how did you know what I was straight away?"

"THAT'S ONLY TWO QUESTIONS." Sage hadn't expected to find the vampire so easily. He'd stopped in for a coffee because he still felt half dead and the headache hadn't given up. Sitting opposite the vampire he didn't feel much better. He kept looking for a hint of fangs behind the man's well-formed lips— that was the only reason he was looking at his mouth.

With the ranch closed people didn't generally just stop into town. When he'd seen the stranger, he'd changed his mind about the coffee to go and had planned on taking a table nearby so he could get a better scent off him. When he'd gotten close, he'd known the man wasn't human. He wasn't a shifter either, though. He had an earthy scent, almost metallic. Something that made him want to go for a run and hunt...with him.

He shuddered but suppressed it. He'd been told to watch the vampire not have breakfast, not chat or play with him. Certainly not to want to run wild with him.

The vampire pushed his plate aside, put his elbows on the table, and laced his fingers. His knuckles were covered in old white scars like he'd been in too many knife fights.

"I already asked your name."

He had, too. Maybe if Sage volunteered his name, the vampire would do the same.

"Sage." He extended his hand.

The vampire didn't take it. "Never offer your hand to a...a man like me."

"Fine." He lowered his hand. What was he missing? The man's eyes looked more like a wolf's than a human. A deep amber, like bourbon. The thought of alcohol turned his stomach, but he couldn't look away. There was something about him that made Sage want to take a closer sniff. He wanted to smell him while as a cougar. He hadn't expected a vampire to be so alive. "But you are, aren't you?"

"Yeah. Is that going to be a problem?"

"Are you going to make it one?"

"I'm here to see family. That's all."

That seemed to be going around. Who was the vampire's family?

"Stay out of trouble." Sage stood. The look the vampire gave him wasn't that of one paranormal assessing another. It was the look a man gave another man. Their gazes clashed and held for that moment too long.

Sage gave a small nod. They had more than one thing in common.

Then he grinned and walked out. Tailing the vampire might be a fun distraction from the gathering at the ranch. Despite the niggling doubt that he was still viewed as the baby, he was going to make the best of his escape from family obligations and daily chores. This was going to be like a holiday.

CHAPTER THREE

SAGE WALKED up the road to his truck, then waited for the vampire to leave the diner. He was betting his life the matt black motorbike was his. No one around here had anything that expensive looking, or clean. Sure enough not even ten minutes later, the vampire left the diner with a carry bag, which he tucked into his jacket before zipping up. He put his helmet and gloves on taking a moment to look around before getting on his bike.

Only after he'd pulled away did Sage start his truck and cautiously follow. There weren't many cars on the road, and he didn't want to be too obvious. Maybe the vampire was telling the truth and visiting family. But as far as Sage knew there were no other vampires in town. There was nothing but cougar shifters for miles. This was their territory and shifters tended to have an area. There wasn't enough of them to worry about over-lap. At least not out here. He couldn't imagine living in the city and running into all kinds of paranormals on a daily basis.

Up ahead the bike turned right. Sage followed, keeping nice and slow. The vampire didn't stop at any of the houses. He kept going past the church, then pulled up at the edge of the cemetery. Sage drove by as though there was somewhere else to go further up. There was a campground if he went a few more miles, but he didn't go that far. He parked and walked back, determined find out who the vampire was visiting. That might give a clue as to who he was.

By the time Sage made it to the cemetery on foot, the vampire was sitting in the grass surrounded by weeds that he'd pulled. He was holding food and talking to the headstone. Sage sniffed and knew it was Sally's cherry pie in the vampire's hands. Sage crouched in the shadows and watched as the vampire carefully put the pie on the grave. What a waste.

Conversation with the dead over the vampire sat there for a few more minutes, eyes closed as though in prayer and untroubled by the sunlight on his face. Shouldn't he be turning to dust or something?

Sage made a mental note to ask the seer about vampire lore. If he was going to be hanging around one, he needed to know how to keep safe. The cross in his pocket might be useless. That wasn't a comforting thought.

Insects buzzed and leaves whispered. Not another sound for miles. They could be the only people in existence. If the vampire ate him, no one would ever know. Fear wasn't something that usually squirmed with in Sage, but out here where the dead were rotting in the ground and the living were too far away should he call for help, it squeezed his heart and made him want to run for the safety of his truck.

He didn't have a gun, but he had a mean hunting knife, a toolbox, and an assortment of wire in the truck. He also had teeth if he had time to shift. If.

He didn't know how fast a vampire could move.

The vampire opened his eyes and turned to stare straight at him. "Are you going to lurk three steps behind me for my entire stay?"

Sage swallowed. He was more than three steps away; more like fifteen yards. Damn the vampire was good. Sage was downwind and all.

He stood with thigh muscles as shaky as a newly born alpaca's. He walked, as casually as he could, to where the vampire waited, wrists resting on his knees like he had nothing to fear.

Cemeteries, Sage hated them. None of his family was buried here. Most were cremated and had a tree planted in their memory in a pretty spot on the property. He shoved his hands into his pockets to hide and quiver. "Don't want you causing trouble."

He looked up at Sage. "Don't you have a family thing to get to?"

"What do you know about that?"

He shrugged. "Don't get your fur all afluff. I only know what the waitress said, that you cats have a thing on."

Sage was tempted to hiss that he wasn't afluff. He wasn't a skittish house cat. But that was exactly how he felt in that moment, even though he was standing, and he'd been the one to sneak up on the vampire...and be called out.

He glanced at the head stone looking for clues. Abigail Gracewell. She'd been dead twenty years. "That your family?"

"Yeah." The vampire stood and dusted the ass of his jeans off.

He wasn't as tall as Sage had expected, barely reaching his nose. But there was something about him that made it hard to look away while at the same time making Sage want to run as far and as fast as he could. The mixed reactions his body was giving was unsettling to say the least. He needed to assess the vampire as a cougar. Maybe as a cougar he could determine what was so troubling. "I'm sorry for your loss."

The vampire pressed his lips together, then he shook his

head as if whatever he was going to say wasn't worth it. "Run home, kitty. Tell them Kirk Gracewell is back."

Kirk Gracewell. He said his name like it should mean something. "Should I know who you are?"

"You won't, but I can guarantee Stone does."

Stone was eight years older. Those years meant nothing as an adult, but that was a big difference as kids. Stone had been a teenager when Sage had been starting first grade.

"Is that a threat?" He stepped closer, hands out of his pocket ready to fight if need be, trying to be braver than he really felt. How dangerous was Kirk? The seer had said watch, not engage, but that moment had passed when he'd joined the vampire for breakfast.

"No. I don't make threats. I'm a hunter like you." The corners of his lips curved up.

In that moment Sage knew they were nothing alike. There was a burning hunger in Kirk's amber eyes that hadn't been there in the diner. He resisted the urge to step back. "What do you want?"

"Justice. Though you might call it revenge." Kirk brushed past, the back of his hand against Sage's for a second and certainly no more, but there was a jolt as though current had passed between them and the world was unstable for a heartbeat.

Sage turned to watch Kirk walk toward the gate. "What are you going to do?"

"Find out the truth."

"The truth about what?"

"My sister's murder." Kirk stood in the gateway, one side with the living the other with the dead.

"If you kill anyone—"

"I only want to kill one person."

At least he was honest about wanting to kill. "Who?"

"I don't know yet."

Kirk believed his sister had been murdered, and the seer had sensed trouble. "Do you think one of us did it?"

He nodded.

Sage shook his head. "We have rules against that."

"Do you? Really?"

"Yes."

Kirk looked away. "I'm sure I'll be running into you again, so I'll see you around."

"Wait." He didn't want the vampire to walk away because then he'd have to go home and talk to the seer and he was fairly sure that he had made a mess of this already. "You can't feed on anyone in town."

Sage was reasonably sure the seer would agree that was a good rule to have. Having a few people wake up with vampire bites would create all kinds of awkward questions.

"If I did, they wouldn't even notice. You didn't." Kirk stepped through the gate.

Sage stared at his hand—the only place Kirk had touched him. There was no mark. There'd been only the slightest sensation. Sage jogged over to the gate, but Kirk was already on his bike and driving away.

———

BEFORE TODAY KIRK had never been to the place where Abby's body had been found. After seeing the silvery cougar attack her, he'd run home. When she hadn't returned, he'd known she wasn't ever coming back. He'd also known that kids without adults ended up in care and he didn't want to be the odd one out in someone else's family. So, in the morning, after staying up all night and expecting the cougar to come after him, he'd caught the bus to the next town as if going to school and kept on going to the city where he could get lost.

He'd read the discarded newspapers and had followed the story, though. He'd almost been tempted to go home for her funeral, but he had no money and he was terrified that the Madison's would realize he was there. They'd dumped her body and the cops claimed it was suicide. Just like Mom.

He parked his bike in the car park and strolled over to the picnic spot. Many of the trees were bare, but in summer it would be pretty. She would've never chosen this spot. Abby was a goth bitch at her best. He smiled, remembering the way she'd painted her nails black, then done his toenails. Their father had yelled from his sick bed that they were both fucked in the head like their mother. Mom told him to shut up.

Two weeks later, Dad had been dead. At the time he'd thought whatever was killing him had finally succeeded. He'd been kind of right, though it had been a few more years before Kirk had realized Mom was just like him.

Mom had come here. Her car had been found in the car park. It had been winter and the river had been full, and she'd cut her wrists and tossed herself in. She left them both letters apologizing.

Abby hadn't copied Mom, no matter how much it appeared that way.

He closed his eyes. The water gurgled, whispering in his ears. The air was sharp and clean, unlike in the city. There it hummed with human energy; here it was something else. Something he couldn't grab. He wasn't a nature witch, but he liked the feel of it. The way it tasted even if it wouldn't nourish him.

At the back of his throat was the taste of Sage. It stuck like a burr in fur, tasting faintly of musk and cinnamon and an undercurrent of something else that wasn't unpleasant just different.

He rubbed the back of his hand where they'd touched for the barest of seconds.

He really needed another taste.

His eyes flicked open. No, he didn't.

While he'd fed on shifters before, it had been accidental when in a summer crowd and skin brushed skin. A thousand tiny tastes to make a meal. Not all pleasant, but it was an easy way to feed without worrying about hurting anyone.

He couldn't touch without feeding. He rubbed his knuckles then cracked them, remembering too well the last time he'd embraced a lover. After that, he'd sworn never again. But the ache to touch and be touched lived beneath his skin, a hunger he could never sate. He shouldn't have touched Sage, but he hadn't been able to resist.

He imagined he could still feel the heat of his hand against his. Still taste the cinnamon on his tongue. The power he'd craved now had him chained. Every day he lost a little more of the things that made life worth living.

Had his mother felt the walls closing in?

Is that why she'd come here?

He followed the trail next to the river, not sure where he was going or what he was doing only that he needed to go to the places Abby had been. There'd be no clues. The cops had found nothing. What had the official words been? Too much damage? Evidence washed away? Animals had nibbled on her before she'd been found downstream.

Abby had never hurt anyone in her entire life. She had a wicked sharp tongue, but she loved her friends and family and would defend them to her last breath. While Abby hadn't been popular, she hadn't been a loner like him either. By the time he'd hit high school he'd known he was different—and not just because he liked guys.

He'd asked Abby about magic and witchcraft once, but

she'd said her stupid spells were just to keep the assholes away, and they had worked. Most of the guys at school liked their chicks blond and vapid, not spiky and mouthy.

Alone in the city he'd used that same bravado.

As an adult he saw it for what it was—a coping mechanism. A mask she could pull up even at home. Mom hated Abby's witch phase. Abby had cursed her after a fight, and Mom had claimed she already was. If she'd known what she was, she hadn't left him any clues or words of wisdom.

He stepped onto the bridge and scanned both sides of the river, but Sage hadn't followed him this time. Kirk almost wished he had. It was too quiet, too isolated.

Abby was dead before she'd even dumped here. He found a measure of peace in that. She hadn't been screaming for help; she'd never gotten a chance. He knew how cougars killed, and a scrawny eighteen-year-old girl who didn't even reach his chin— and he wasn't tall by any stretch—stood no chance. He leaned on the railing and hung his head.

The guilt that he'd carried for so long had been released, but the sadness that his family had fallen apart so easily was much harder to let go. Like his mother, anyone Kirk got close to would eventually die. He'd gotten the bad gene, or whatever caused this, from her. Her guilt had driven her to this bridge.

Like her, he belonged nowhere. And never would.

CHAPTER FOUR

SAGE'S TRUCK roared up the driveway. He turned right toward the main house to park, but his spot—not that it was his officially, but he used it because he was the one doing the day to day running—had been taken by a red sports car that looked like someone was trying too hard.

He growled, shoved the truck into reverse, and parked next to the barn on the grass. He was sick of this gathering already. Somehow, he'd remembered them as being more fun. Last time he'd been twenty and no one had expected much from him. He certainly hadn't expected much from the gathering. And he hadn't been hoping to be the next familiar chosen. He wasn't hoping this time either, but there were some he didn't want receiving the honor because they were already over inflated.

But if it were him, his place in the family would be cemented. His siblings might stop seeing him as the loser who'd stayed behind. The baby who couldn't leave home. He didn't want to leave home...except for now when it was full of strangers who were mostly related to him somehow. Second cousin twice removed; he couldn't work that out even if it was explained to him twice a day.

He got out and slammed the car door.

"You managed to palm your jobs off." Stone put the feed he was carrying down and walked over.

"I had things to do." Did he smell like diner and cemetery and Kirk? He kept his distance. "Besides it'll do you good to get your hands dirty."

Stone would know Kirk, apparently. The question was on the tip of his tongue, but the seer's warning was still echoed. *Tell no one.*

She knew more than she'd told him, which wasn't unusual.

Stone scowled. "What's wrong?"

"Nothing. I just got a list of things I have to do for other people. I'm the seer's bitch at the moment." He tried to brush it off so Stone wouldn't ask more questions. If it were Clay, he'd keep digging and he knew how to ask to get what he wanted.

Stone laughed, then stopped as though he knew something was amiss. "What's she got you doing?"

"Buying chocolate and vodka." The lie tumbled off his lips. "But I think she just wants you lot to get in touch with the ranch again."

If any of them wanted to come back, Sage wasn't going to be happy. He liked his brothers well enough, but the cousins they'd ran with not so much. The cousins on the other side of the family were more his kind of people, but he was about five years too old for them. He was the odd one out, his mother's surprise baby from a fling. Apparently, at the time it had been quite the scandal, even though her husband had died in a car accident when Stone was a baby.

Stone pulled a face. "I don't mind helping out; you helped me enough when you were knee high. But this is so not my thing."

"I know. How are the plans for increasing the accommodation going?" After they'd agreed to expand, Sage left that kind of paperwork to Stone and Clay.

"We'll go for a ride later. Mom wants us to work it out. I get the feeling she leaves it all to you?"

"Yeah. That a problem?" His brothers had a share in the business, but Sage got a wage and a share. This was his place and if his brothers wanted to cash out, he would be screwed.

"No. You're doing good. Don't let anyone tell you otherwise." Stone smiled. "Better take the seer her goodies."

"Yeah." Except he had no goodies in his truck. Still he walked around and reached in, hoping he at least had a bag he could carry or that his brother would walk away.

Stone leaned on the door and peered in. "You didn't go into town to buy Violet anything. You are the worst liar."

Sage glared at his brother and seethed at the seer for putting him in this position.

"It's fine. It's cute that she's covering for you. But you know what Ash is like so maybe tell your boyfriend to chill until the gathering is over."

Sage rolled his eyes. "I don't have a boyfriend."

The smile left Stone's face and was replaced with something much worse. Pity. Not this again. He didn't need a partner to be happy.

"It's fine." Sage slammed the door shut.

"Clearly it's not."

"What do you want me to say?"

"I don't know. I want you to be happy. We grew up and left but..." He glanced at the ground and scuffed his boot. "You didn't have that choice."

"Yeah, I did. Don't get the guilts because I stayed. I like it here." But the dating scene wasn't much even without the added complication of being a gay shifter. "I still meet people."

Of course the only interesting person he'd met lately was a vampire, which was rather telling.

"I don't need details." But Stone smiled and pressed, "Look, if you want a week in the city, we'll house swap and I'll take care of things here."

"Too many people. Where do you shift?" He shrugged. He didn't think he could handle the city. But Stone had met his wife there. There were places where shifters gathered.

It was only when he was surrounded by people that Sage felt lonely. Most of the time he didn't care that he was single and had only had a handful of short-term boyfriends. Some liked the idea of a cowboy for a boyfriend but not the reality of driving down from the city every weekend, or they expected him to drive up not understanding the alpacas didn't take weekends off and some of the work was too heavy for Mom.

Others, Sage couldn't tell the truth to and secrets became a thing between them. But how did he break it to a human boyfriend that he wasn't entirely human? And if they knew, they could tell people. It was too dangerous. What he needed was another paranormal.

Kirk with his amber eyes and barely there smile flashed through his mind.

He did *not* need a vampire.

"Just think about it okay. It would be good for the kids to come here now they're bigger," Stone said.

"You're welcome anytime."

Stone wrinkled his nose. "Not the same when it's full of tourists—though that was a brilliant idea," he added in a rush.

"Different when it's full of *family*, too. Are all the chores done?"

"Yeah. Do you plan on slacking off the whole time?"

"You'd have to ask the seer. She's the one pulling my strings."

Something flickered across Stone face, before being replaced with a smile. "I think I'll leave that be."

That was probably a wise choice.

Sage trudged up to the house, took his boots off in the mud room, and then padded through in his socks. He froze and turned just as his mother pounced. She pulled him into a hug.

"Don't sneak up on me." His heart was pounding even though he knew it was a friendly attack.

"I need the practice."

She came hunting with him less and less, content to loll in the moonlight. The words were on the tip of his tongue, but he didn't say it. "Are you going out for a run with Stone and Clay while they're here?"

She drew away. "I can't keep up with them. Besides they're grown up with their own families." She ruffled his hair messing it up. "You're still my cub."

Except he wasn't. But he didn't argue since she had that look in her eyes.

"Stone would like it. He's talking about bringing his kids down for a week sometime while I go up there." It was the wrong thing to say.

Mom's face fell. "Oh...I thought you liked—"

"Like a holiday, Mom. This will always be home." He gave her a quick hug. "Are Mica and Ash being tools?" Whenever his cousins returned, they always stirred up trouble.

She stiffened. "I can handle them."

"Maybe next time we don't invite them." Stone and Clay would ask why, but Sage doubted anyone else would. The bad blood hadn't dissipated with time; it had hardened into an ever-present air of resentment that this land should've been theirs.

"What's that scent on you?" She inhaled again. "Did you sneak out for pancakes? I'd have made you some."

"I had errands and I got hungry." He drew away before she

smelled the metallic vampire scent on him. Today was not going well. "I need an aspirin." He took a few steps then turned. "Do you still have the old school year books?"

"I think they're in Ash's old room."

Even though his cousins hadn't lived on the ranch in over two decades the designations had stuck. Usually the extra rooms were empty, the house too big for just Mom and Sage. With everyone here the house and external guest houses were full.

Ash's room had become a filing/library/record room. The tiny office downstairs couldn't keep all the paperwork—and there was more of it now that they were open to the public.

"Why?" Mom's eyebrows drew down as though trying to figure out what was going on just by staring.

He looked away and shrugged. "You know how it is online when someone says they went to the same school, but you don't remember them."

"If you can't smell them. you shouldn't trust them."

"I'll keep that in mind. Violet upstairs?"

"Yes, but she said she had *work*."

Sage wasn't sure if his mother meant seer work or if Violet was drawing. He figured he'd leave her alone for the moment and check out Kirk's claim.

Ash's room had shelves against all the walls and beneath the window was a bank of filing cabinets. Sage was sure they were keeping too many records, some over thirty years old, but he knew why Mom wouldn't throw them out. They had her husband's handwriting on them.

Even though he'd been dead for years before Sage was born, for a long time he'd been the man Sage considered his father simply because his brothers had and there was no one else. No one explained it until he was old enough to understand the rumors. His biological father was a shifter who'd answered an ad for summer work. He'd stayed at the ranch for a few months before leaving; Sage's brothers barely remembered him. Sage doubted the man even knew he had a son.

He scanned the shelves, past the farming almanacs and books on alpacas that he'd had memorized before he'd been a senior. Down on the bottom of the shelf near the filing cabinet was a small stack of high school yearbooks. He ignored his own and grabbed the ones Stone would be in. He leafed through, not sure if he wanted Kirk to be telling the truth or lying.

Gracewell, Kirk. There he was. Unsmiling. His hair had been shoulder-length then; now it was close cropped like he couldn't be bothered with a proper haircut either way.

Sage closed his eyes and tried to recall the dates on the headstone. Abby was older than Kirk. He grabbed Ash's book, but she wasn't there.

"You're back already."

Sage startled as Violet walked in. "Yeah, I had to check somethings out. Besides it was weird following him around. I'm not a stalker. Not *that* kind of stalker anyway. I'm not following him as a cougar."

Violet sat on the floor next to him. "What did you find out?"

He handed over the book and pointed to Kirk. "I spoke with him."

She didn't look up, her gaze intent on the black and white photo. "Did you? What did he have to say?"

"He visited his sister's grave. Abigail Gracewell." He lowered his voice. "He thinks one of us killed her." He wanted Violet to laugh and denounce the idea. It was ridiculous.

Violet looked up sharply. Sage expected a denial, or a promise to run the troublemaking vampire out of town. Anything except silence. With every passing second his

THE VAMPIRE'S FAMILIAR   33

stomach fell. Kirk had been telling the truth and the seer knew
something.

"What else did he say?" Her face was perfectly serious as
though she believed one of them could've killed Abigail.

No. His cousins and the others could be pains but they
weren't killers. "You believe the vampire?"

"I think it's possible, and you need to look into it."

Sage blinked, unable to take her stare. "He's here for
revenge. To kill the cougar responsible."

"If the killer got away, it could be called justice."

"He said something similar. You know who Abigail was."
There was something else going on, but he didn't know what.

"I didn't know her. But I know of the Gracewell family."
She smiled and seamlessly shifted topics. "Tell me about the
vampire. I've never met one."

Sage hesitated, but he needed to know more about
vampires and telling Violet would be the quickest route to
answers. So, he told her about the brief touch and Kirk's claim
that he'd fed on Sage. "Have I lost a year of my life or
something?"

"Not that much. He's an energy vampire. If he touched you
for longer and took more, you'd end up sick and exhausted for a
time, but you'd recover. Did he have marks?" She touched her
hand.

"On his knuckles. I thought it was from fighting at first, but
they were too clean."

"He's been trained. They use them to control how much
they take. The marks make them stronger."

Sage scowled. "I thought you'd never met one."

"I haven't but somethings you just learn."

Vampires had never been part of *his* curriculum. "So, what
now?"

Violet considered him for a moment and then said, "I suggest you help him."

"What?" Watching a vampire was a very different thing to helping one. Especially one that want to kill one of his family in retaliation. "I can't help him." Not without betraying a member of his family. But was it betrayal if they had killed Abigail?

She leaned in closer. "If one of us killed his sister and got away with it, who's to say he hasn't killed again and that there is a serial killer in our midst?"

"But we protect ourselves." Family came first. That had been drilled into him from the time he could talk. That, and they didn't discuss what they were.

"And in killing a human, they didn't think about the rest of us."

That was true, but this was still something he didn't feel comfortable with. Hunting down killers was Clay's thing. He was the cop. The seer knew that, yet she still wanted Sage to do it, which meant that she'd seen something. "How am I supposed to help him? Should I ask who remembers her?"

Violet's eyebrows rose in horror. "No. That would not be safe."

It was then Sage realized how troubled the seer really was. How afraid. She was sure there was a killer on the ranch. "What have you seen?"

She clasped his hand. "Trust me when I say, keep this to yourself. That may not be enough," she muttered almost to herself.

The hairs on the back of his neck spiked and cold trickled down his spine. "What do you mean? Is Kirk dangerous?"

"Not to you...but others are."

She'd sent him to tail Kirk, and if the killer knew what Sage was doing, he was in danger. Annoyance flared, but he kept it locked down as best he could. Violet was trying to help—who, he wasn't sure. "You've put me in the crosshairs."

"You were on that path anyway. I just got you there quicker, so you have more time to stop this. Only you can." Her gaze was intense.

He wanted to yank his hand away and refuse. He wasn't a Madison; this wasn't his problem. This would only push him further to the edge with those who already resented him. "Why only me?"

"I can't say."

"Can't or won't?"

"Both." She released his hands and stood smoothly. "It's not good to know too much about the future. It can be a terrible thing."

CHAPTER FIVE

KIRK PARKED his bike near the B&B. The house had been done up since he'd last seen it. When he'd driven through this morning, he'd thought the town hadn't changed at all. It still had that small town, raise your family here vibe with just enough for young families, not enough to keep teens interested. The next town over was bigger and the city only a few hours' drive. He hadn't appreciated how safe Madison Gully was until he'd been on his own in the city. But the town had changed in small ways. New signs hung above old shops. Houses had been renovated. More houses built.

At the street level the Madisons still commanded respect. He'd seen it when Sage had walked into the diner. Everyone knew who they were, and everyone owed the Madison ranch for their jobs and their town. Even if they didn't openly acknowledge it, everyone knew if the ranch went down so did the town.

Kirk had no doubt the Madison's would close ranks and protect whichever one of them killed Abby. He checked for his tail, but Sage must have scampered home to make a report.

Evil vampire had pancakes and visited his sister's grave. Oh, and he thinks one of us killed her.

For half a second he regretted telling the truth, but he figured the Madison most troubled by his presence would wind up at his door, which would make finding the killer that much easier. While he knew what the killer looked like as a cat, he didn't know him as a man.

He should've been earlier that night. If Abby and he had been together...

The old guilt was still there, smaller now after decades of wear, but he couldn't put it down completely.

He got his bag out of the compartment on the back of the bike and walked around to the front door. He knocked and a young woman opened it.

"Hi, I'm Kirk Gracewell, I've booked a room." He smiled, hoping he didn't look threatening in his leather jacket. His helmet was tucked under his arm and his backpack slung over his shoulder. He'd packed light, not wanting to be here for long. After killing a Madison they'd all be after him.

"Yes. Come through. You're a bit early; I was just doing some baking."

She got him signed in quickly as he'd already paid online when he'd booked. He'd left booking until the last moment, trying to resist the lure, but knowing that he couldn't leave the promised unfilled. He'd spent last night in the next town over, coming to grips with what he was planning. Getting justice for Abby would put a target on his back. But he owed Abby, and he wasn't stupid enough to ignore the need to be here. His past needed to be settled. Then he could move on.

And if the Coven found out what he'd done?

He wished he'd ridden in, done what needed to be done, and left without anyone knowing who he was or what he was. Now they'd all know. Maybe Sage was calling the

Coven now. That was almost a good idea, because then they'd have to investigate Abby's death properly. She'd still get her justice. But it would be at the cost of his life. The Coven wouldn't let a vampire go free. He cracked his knuckles.

The woman smiled but watched him intently. "Just down the hall, room number three. Breakfast will be available between seven and nine. If you need anything just give me a call. Is there anything you need now?"

Something she was baking smelled delicious. Or maybe it was her and she'd taste like fresh bread if he touched her hand as he took his key. It would be bad form to feed on his host, though. At least on the first day.

"If I need more than two nights will I be able to extend my stay?"

"That shouldn't be a problem, we're usually quite this time of year. A bit cold for those wanting to visit the ranch."

"Yeah, it's closed. I'd hoped to go riding." He barely knew which end of the horse was front, but he wanted to hear the gossip regarding the Madison family.

She nodded. "Family thing. Mom said they do it every ten years. They all come in from out of town. It's kind of cute; probably easier to do now than over Christmas."

And because they all stayed at the ranch, he wouldn't be able to get a list of names from her. He knew a handful from school, but that was all. He needed to know who was staying there and who'd been there twenty years ago.

The woman kept talking. "I'm sure if you really wanted to go riding, Sage would take you. He runs the ranch and often pops into town." She reached beneath the counter and pulled out a brochure. "Here you go. This has some of the trails and the costs and his number."

That was exactly what he needed.

"Thank you." Kirk upped the wattage on his smile. "Got one for fishing?"

He could fish. He'd often spent summer at the river catching what would become dinner. And since he was playing the part of tourist, he might as well do it properly.

"Sure. There's a camping and fishing store just next to the hardware store." She handed over another piece of paper.

And Kirk was willing to bet the hardware store was still owned by the Peters family.

"I'll give you one with hiking trails, too. It's cold and there's less people, but you don't strike me as the kind of guy who's bothered too much by things like that."

He gave her a guilty shrug like she had him pegged. "You got me. I do prefer to holiday in the off seasons." He didn't really holiday at all. He worked as an orderly in the biggest hospital, kept shitty hours, and lived quietly to avoid drawing attention to what he was. If the Coven learned he existed, they'd send someone to end him. His mentor had drilled that fear into him, so Kirk knew coming here was dangerous. But not coming here would be worse. His gut was at odds with his mind.

The brain could be tricked, but the gut didn't lie. Another one of his mentor's favorite lessons. Had his mentor's gut instinct warned him that Kirk's last visit wasn't a social call?

"I hope you have a good stay. I'll see you about. Oh, and if you're looking for a good meal on a budget, I recommend the Old Gully Bar."

"Thanks." He took his brochures and went down the corridor to his room.

It was just like the photos online complete with a view of the backyard through glass doors that opened onto a veranda. He didn't bother unpacking; there wasn't much in his bag to take out and if he needed to leave in a hurry, he didn't want to have to pack. But he did take a seat outside in the swinging chair and read the brochures. He studied the maps of the horse trails and the hiking trails, looking for one that would take him from town to the ranch.

There wasn't one, but the trails joined up with the bridge on the way out of town where they then went in all directions. One followed the river to where he'd been earlier today. Another ran parallel to the road.

He returned his attention to the ranch. From the bridge there were two looping trails that both swept past the edge of the ranch. From there he'd be able to prowl through the paddocks and set up a spot to count cougars. Though he hoped it wouldn't come to that. If he was caught trespassing, there'd be consequences.

———

Sage added some wood chips to the barbeque. It already smelled good and the meat had only been on a few hours. The kids ran around, burning off excess energy. Most weren't old enough to shift, yet. At the next gathering they would be. He remembered being ten, and watching the older cousins go off in cougar form to play in the moonlight while he had to go to bed. At twenty he'd been able to join in, stripping and shifting and slinking through the shadows.

This time he was expected to be responsible and offer insights about shifting to the younger ones. The queer ones. He got sympathetic head shakes at his lack of partner from older relatives.

And next time, when he was forty?

He tossed another chip onto the fire and watched it burn.

He didn't really want to be thinking about doing this again in ten years. The single uncle who worked the ranch. While half of that wasn't bad, the other half was terrifying. As much as he didn't want to admit that Stone was right, Sage did get lonely, and not in the way that could be solved by having over thirty of his closest family members turn up.

The ranch felt crowded even though not everyone came anymore. Some didn't care about the seer's announcement of who the next familiar would be. They no longer believed that a strong pack needed a witch, or they didn't want it to be them, so they stayed away thinking to avoid fate. For as long as Sage could remember, the announcement had always been made on the last night of the gathering. Last time, he'd been dreading it. He didn't want it to be him because the idea of tying his life to another person—someone he didn't even really know—was abhorrent. Even now he wasn't sure...but the idea that there was someone fated for him had an appeal he couldn't shake.

If it was meant to be, that made it easy. Didn't it?

It wouldn't be him, though. To be a familiar, one needed to meet a witch and there needed to be a certain magic between them. He wished the woman who'd been selected last time was here so he could ask her how she'd ended up meeting her witch. They were now married.

His cousin Ash strolled over, interrupting Sages thoughts. "Where did you disappear to this morning? I had to put feed in bins."

"Troughs," Sage corrected. "And I had other errands to run. More people means more work even though you're all family." This was no different to peak tourist season with long days, but he liked that more because he didn't have time to think about anything else. And at least tourists didn't quiz him about his personal life.

Ash shook his head. "I don't know how you put up with tourists. Dad would've hated so many strangers crawling over Madison land."

Sage lifted an eyebrow. Mica and Ash had made a few grumbles last night, but Sage had put it down to the liquor and bitterness that they were now interlopers. This wasn't their land and hadn't been in a long time. "Tourism seemed like a smart second income."

"Why do you care about the fortunes of the ranch? You aren't even a Madison."

Sage clamped his jaw closed. Ash was older, but Sage was taller, and he wasn't out of shape. If it came to a fight, he wouldn't be copping the worst of it. "I was raised a Madison even if it isn't in my blood."

"We don't even know your bloodline." Ash stepped closer. "This ranch isn't yours, boy."

Sage held his cousin's stare. "Your dad wanted to be bought out and he was. He left and took you and Mica with him. My brothers and I worked our blood and sweat into the soil. They wanted to pursue other careers, and I wanted to stay, so it worked out well. Would you be having this conversation with Stone or Clay if they were the ones working the ranch?"

"Dad made a mistake."

"Your dad tried to force Mom off the land. He got his bluff called." And Ash's dad was dead. Had been for a few years.

Ash's lips drew back. "This ranch belongs to the Madison bloodline. You and your Mom don't belong." His lips twisted into a cruel smirk. "And we all know you aren't going to produce any heirs." Ash shoved Sage's shoulder.

Sage snarled, a low warning growl that made his ribs vibrate. "Clay and Stone have kids—Madison blood, since that matters to you." He leaned a little closer. "Mom buying your dad out was the best thing that could've happened."

Ash lifted his hand and curled his fingers.

"Sage, I need your assistance." Violet's voice cut across the brewing fight.

"Run along, boy. When she makes me familiar, I'll come for the ranch."

"You don't have the funds or the balls to go for Stone and Clay. That's why you're ragging on me." He stepped back. "The ranch isn't for sale for any price."

He took a few more steps back, never taking his eyes off Ash. It would be really nice if that branch of the family could be disinvited. It wouldn't happen, though. This get together was open to all. When he'd put a few yards between them he spun and walked toward Violet.

Her lips were pursed, and her eyes were narrowed. Sage was sure the only reason Ash didn't jump him from behind was because she was watching. "How can I help?"

"You need to go back to town."

He kept his face neutral, but he wanted to roll his eyes and ask why. How was he supposed to find out who killed Abigail if he was with Kirk? "I don't see how that's going to help. The killer is probably here."

"More reason for you to be in town." She took his hands and kept her voice low. "You need to solve this before others work out who Kirk is."

"My absence is being noted."

Her gaze flicked to Ash. "They can deal with it."

It was him who had to deal with it, though.

"What did Ash want?" Violet asked.

He shrugged and considered brushing off her question, then decided against it. If the seer wanted him to work for her, she could do something for him. "The ranch...there's no way he could make a claim is there? If Ash or Mica were to get a witch, could they take it?"

Violet shook her head. "Maybe once, but these days everything is legal, and the deeds are safe in your mother's name.

You and your brothers are in the will. Ash and Mica have no claim."

"But they would've, once." He needed to know, in case they went to the Coven and invoked some kind of archaic rule.

She nodded, confirming his fear. "The ranch used to be run by the Madison with a witch. But we haven't done that in over a hundred years. Passing ownership around like that doesn't work these days." It didn't sit well in his gut and it must have shown in his face. "Listen to me when I say the ranch is safe. No one is throwing your mom off."

He wanted to believe her, but if Ash or Mica became a familiar, they did have a claim. "But you're throwing me off."

He wasn't a Madison by blood. Not even a drop. If anyone shouldn't be at the gathering it was him.

"You have a job to do, Sage."

"Can't you just see who did it?" Sage didn't want to believe a killer was staying at the ranch. Maybe Violet was wrong, and Kirk was a liar. But Violet didn't make mistakes. When she spoke, it was because she knew enough to be sure.

Violet's gaze settled on Ash, who was still loitering by the barbeque and watching them. "It doesn't work that way. I can't see the past. Even the future can be muddy. I do what I can to keep people out of trouble. Sometimes it's not enough."

"Where do I start, if I can't ask questions here? Should I go to the cops and find out what they know?"

She considered him for a moment and then nodded. "Yes. That's a good place to start. And talk to your vampire."

He's not my vampire.

One touch and he was dinner. The hairs on his arm prickled as though remembering, but the touch had felt like nothing more than a bit of static between them. He didn't feel older or weaker. He didn't feel any different at all. "How do I stop him from feeding on me?"

"You can't."

"Great." He was going to end up as a vampire snack and the seer was almost smiling about it. He hated her games. Clay would be so much better at this. "I'll be in town if you need me. Am I allowed to come home to sleep?"

"I'm not forcing you to go. But what is coming will happen whether you're ready or not."

"He'll get justice?" That was all Kirk wanted, to know who killed his sister. But that wouldn't be the end of it. Kirk wanted blood for blood. Sage couldn't hate him for that but that didn't mean he had to like it either.

"Blood will be spilled. You control whose and how much." She said it in a way that made his marrow turn to snow. If he did nothing, people would get hurt. If he helped Kirk, he'd be exposing one of his family as a killer.

What if it was one of his brothers?

CHAPTER SIX

KIRK TOOK the hostess up on the suggestion of dinner at the Old Gully Bar. It was the kind of place that immediately felt cozy and welcoming. He took a small corner table that was tucked out of the way and ordered himself a bottle of red wine and a steak—things he could've only dreamed about eating the last time he was in town.

Truthfully, things he hadn't been able to afford until five years ago.

He sipped the wine, glad he could still enjoy alcohol, and pulled out the notebook he'd started after he'd gotten off the streets. The first half was filled with angry rantings about his father, his mother, and the man who killed Abby. There was blood smeared on the pages from when his mentor had carved the sigils into his skin and he'd written with pride about his magic. He'd been such a young fool.

If he'd been braver, he might have made a few pages about his mentor in here. But he hadn't, partly out of fear the man could read his mind and partly because he was sure this journal had been read on more than one occasion.

When he was eighteen, he'd gone to the library and made

copies of the newspaper articles about Abby's *suicide*, printed them out, and stuck them in. He hadn't known what to do back then. He hadn't even understood what he could do, only that he had a hunger food couldn't sate and a mentor who wanted him to bring shifters home. Later as his writing and thoughts had gotten more controlled, he'd realized his mother was just like him. Unfortunately he'd only realized that after he'd let himself be picked up in a bar. It had been going really well until the other guy nearly lost consciousness before they'd even gotten their clothes off. Despite his fear of what he'd done Kirk had crackled with energy all the way home.

He'd eaten his lover. And that had been the last time he'd been with anyone.

That night he'd tried to burn the marks off his hands so he could go back to who he'd been, to being able to touch another without killing them. The bitter truth was, he'd always been like this, but it had grown stronger as he'd gotten older. He'd sat like stone as the sigils were carved into the scar tissue. He needed the sigils to control the flow of energy, but he couldn't stop it. Every time he touched someone; he took a little of their life. He hadn't gotten the grades to be a doctor like he'd wanted, and he'd given up on being a nurse, too. He couldn't help people only kill them. So, he got a job as an orderly and discovered he could feed off freshly spilled blood.

He was vampire, just like his mother. She'd killed their father with her love. He didn't know if Abby was the same, but none of her boyfriends had ever dropped dead.

Energy snapped across the room, and a pull he couldn't resist following made him look up. The kitty was back. It took Sage exactly four seconds to locate him, and again he made his way over as if they were old friends. Sage smiled and took the spare seat at the table like it had been left for him.

"This is dinner for one." Kirk closed the notebook. There

were no clues to be found in there, only the anger of a confused teen discovering he was a monster.

"The waitress will come and take my order in a moment. What are you having?"

"Steak." Kirk really didn't want company, and certainly not Sage who would report everything straight back to his family. Given the lack of pitchforks at his door, maybe he hadn't said anything yet.

"I'll get that, too. Keep it easy." Sage picked up the bottle of wine. "Do you mind?"

"I'm sorry, when did I say you could join me?"

"When you told me about your sister." Sage poured himself a glass and took a sip. "You need my help."

Kirk didn't need anyone, and he'd spent the last few years proving that. People who got close to him tended to die. "I don't."

"I know the names of everyone staying there." Sage took another sip of wine. "And while I don't want to help you, I don't want a killer running free."

Having Sage's insight would make things go quicker, and it didn't mean Kirk had to trust him. "Fine, but we don't have to do dinner."

The waitress walked over and put bread on the table, then took Sage's order. She smiled at Sage like she hoped that he might change his mind about liking men. What she wanted for herself was in Sage's eyes and on his lips when he looked at Kirk; it lasted for a heartbeat before being shuttered. The man was an open book. One Kirk couldn't take the time to read.

"Won't someone notice and care if you spend all your free time hanging around me?" Sage's attention would attract more. While Kirk needed to figure out which cougar it was, he didn't know if Sage would be a help or a hindrance. He certainly couldn't go sneaking about if the kitty was following him, and it made the risk of a set up that much more likely.

"Look, I don't really want to be helping you, but I get the feeling that if you don't find out who it was, then you might take it out on everyone."

"I would not." Not now. When the rage had been burning, he might have considered setting fire to the whole ranch, but he'd been too piss scared to return. Then he'd been taken in by his mentor and his life hadn't been his anymore. The rules were strict, and he had to obey if he wanted to learn the secrets of magic and become powerful. So, he'd bided his time and let himself be turned into this.

He wasn't easy to kill, and he was harder to love. Unlike Sage he had no family. No one gave damn. He wouldn't let himself regret the choices he'd made twenty years ago, because that was a path that lead only to bitterness. Now he had a chance to put things right and move on.

"I expected you lot to close ranks."

Sage nodded. "Yeah, me too. But here I am. And I spoke to the now retired Davy Greenwood, who was a cop around the time."

"I saw the reports. No one wanted to know the truth." Doubts had been raised and quickly swept aside to get the case closed.

"Abby dated his son for a bit, so he knew her. He said she wasn't that kind of girl; she felt responsible for you, being her little brother and all. It didn't seem right, but there were no other clues. No witnesses."

Kirk studied the way the light reflected on his glass. There had been a witness, but he'd run. "If I'd stayed and told the truth, I'd be dead."

No one would've believed him and the shifter responsible would've made sure he stopped speaking. He hadn't had any magic back then, or if he had it was so small, he hadn't noticed. What teenage boy wasn't always hungry?

Their steaks arrived and Kirk breathed in the scent. He let the anticipation build in his mouth and enjoyed the rumble of his stomach.

"You can't each much, can you? You left a perfectly good pile of pancakes uneaten."

He sighed. "You're kind of ruining the moment for me."

"Better than sex?" Sage said with a smile.

Kirk stabbed his steak and cut off a small piece. "Yes."

Then he put it in his mouth determined to ignore the cougar opposite him who was digging into his meal with enthusiasm, knowing that there would be plenty more in his future. Kirk closed his eyes to savor the frission of energy in the rare steak, the taste of blood and meat and the charring of the grill. A happy moan lodged in his throat. He missed being able to eat a whole meal.

"Oh my God, you're serious."

Kirk finished chewing and swallowed, then he opened his eyes. "Yes."

"Is it because..." Sage gave a pointed glance at Kirk's scarred hands.

"Can we just eat?" He wanted to make the most of eating while he could.

"Do you not go on dates with people? Dinners out?"

"No. It's easier not to make friends." Easier for everyone if he didn't start what couldn't be continued.

"But you want to?" Sage pressed.

"It doesn't matter what I want. I can't help what I am."

"And your sister? Was she the same as you?"

Gay, a vampire, a recluse? He wanted to ask but didn't because he knew Sage was asking about the vampire part. "I don't know. I don't think so." He took a drink of wine. "I'm sure my mother was, though."

Sage frowned and returned his attention to his meal. Which gave Kirk the time to enjoy a few more bites of his before his stomach gave that over-burdened twinge. If he kept eating, he'd have to sleep like a snake digesting an overly big meal. Guess that was where the vampires sleeping like the dead myth came from.

He put his cutlery down, so he wouldn't be tempted to take another bite. It was a very nice steak. Even the chips were good, though he'd only allowed himself one, not wanting to waste the small amount he could eat on them.

"Are you done?" Sage glanced hopefully at the steak.

"You can have it." He nudged his plate over, not wanting it to go to waste. Sage lifted the steak and put it on his own plate. Kirk watched him eat for a few moments before he realized how weird that might seem. But he liked looking at Sage a bit too much. Having dinner with him was a bad idea.

Sage looked up and swallowed. "Are you actually watching me eat?"

"Sorry." Kirk picked up his wine and tried not to look at the man opposite.

"No...it's okay. But if one of my brothers is watching that closely it's because they're about to steal food off my plate. Do you want the steak back?"

Yes. He wanted to be able to eat a whole plate of food without making himself ill. "No. I physically can't eat anymore."

"That sucks."

"Yeah." He'd grown up thinking his mother had sacrificed her meals so everyone else could eat but had since learned that wasn't the reason. "Eventually I won't be able to eat at all."

Sage looked devastated on his behalf. "But eating is...it's life."

No food and no sex. Kirk didn't know what he was going to do when that happened. Maybe the real reason his mother had killed herself was because there was nothing left for her to enjoy. His mentor hadn't, though. He'd became more convinced of his own power and had scoured the streets for shifters to feed on—believing they were superior and wanting that special one that would give him more power.

"Not for everyone." And except for times like this, Kirk liked the changes. His eyesight was better during the day and at night, his reflexes were faster, and he healed quickly, especially after feeding.

Sage finished his meal in silence. Then he sipped his wine and studied Kirk before speaking. "Why didn't you come back sooner? Why wait twenty years?"

"I was fifteen. I thought about going to the cops or going out to the ranch to demand justice, but who would've believed me? The cops wouldn't have. And I figured if I went to the ranch I'd never leave. Then I wasn't allowed to leave; my mentor forbade it." The night Abby was killed had been his first real taste of magic. He'd never forget the way the way the killer's energy tasted at the back of his throat.

He hadn't forgotten Abby, but he'd convinced himself that he needed to master his power. He'd been thinking about coming back and feeding off every Madison; now all he wanted was the one who'd killed her. He was glad he'd waited. Coming back young and full of rage would've been far too destructive. Another paranormal would've reported him and the Coven would've turned up and killed him.

"I also had to wait until your family gathered. I knew it was time to return." He touched just below his sternum.

Sage nodded, a faint smile on his lips. "I'm missing a family barbeque to be here."

"Then be with them. You have family. But if you stop me from finding out who killed Abby..." He moved his hand toward where Sage's rested on his wine glass but made sure their skin didn't touch.

Sage's smile turned bitter. "I was raised to believe that family came first. But I also learned early I wasn't really a Madison. My mom raised me to do the right thing, and the seer wants the person found. I think I need to be here." He stretched his fingers and their skin connected.

Cinnamon burst on Kirk's tongue. He drew back as though burned. "Don't do that."

"You don't scare me."

"I should." He could kill with a touch—a prolonged touch but a touch all the same. And yet he wanted Sage to touch his hand again. Not to feed, not even to taste him even though his energy was nice—like hot cookies still on the tray, begging to be eaten even though they'd burn. Kirk wanted more even though he knew he shouldn't, but it had been so long since someone had touched him. His skin craved the contact. He softened his voice. "I don't want to hurt you."

"It doesn't hurt."

"It will." Maybe they could hold hands for a few seconds, maybe ten if Kirk was really careful, but then Sage would weaken, sicken, and hate him.

"So, control how much you take." Sage's fingers brushed the scars on Kirk's knuckles.

Kirk glanced up at the ceiling. "I am. But I can't stop it from happening. All I can do is reduce the flow from you to me to a trickle." When he opened the dam and took all of the energy in, it was like being drunk and dizzy. He could feel and see the pulse of the world and the ribbons of energy. His vision became too bright, every living thing had an aura he could touch and taste, and in those moments it was as though he could do anything.

He couldn't do anything, though. All that energy and magic, and he couldn't do anything useful with it. It was a waste. His mentor didn't think so; the magic gave them a longer life after all. And maybe it had, but Kirk had ended it. Drained the old man dry, until he was too feeble to do anything but to fight for each breath. Then he'd called emergency to report his mentor was having trouble breathing.

He'd watched the man die before the ambulance came, not knowing if he'd done the right thing, but at least his mentor could no longer prey on street kids for meals. Kirk had been the sole beneficiary of the will. His motorbike had been the only luxury he'd allowed himself.

Now as Sage traced the shapes of the archaic letters—their meaning lost with his mentor—Kirk couldn't pull away. "Why are you doing this?"

Was Sage like any cat and just toying with his prey? But the shifter's face was open and honest. There was nothing sly hiding in his gaze.

"Curiosity. And I like the way the scars feel. There's a hum in them that your other skin doesn't have."

"Do you like dying?"

Sage shook his head. "It's almost like you're running your hand along my back."

Kirk closed his eyes and let that image take hold. Sage lying face down and naked on the bed, while Kirk smoothed his hands down his back and over his ass. He'd barely had the chance to discover another's body before that pleasure had been taken. The digestion issue had started soon after.

"When I'm a cougar," Sage whispered the last word and the image fell apart.

Kirk opened his eyes. Petting a cat was very different to what he'd been thinking. It was safer to remember Sage was a cougar, though. He was one of them—a Madison. For all Kirk knew, he'd protect the killer.

Kirk pulled his hand away and missed the contact immediately. "I'm dangerous."

"So am I." Sage smiled and took a sip of wine, his gaze never leaving Kirk.

Kirk pressed his lips together and tried to shove down the awakened desire, but with Sage so close, and the taste of him on his tongue, he couldn't. If he reached out...

He didn't.

He had to focus on the reason he was here, not the reason he'd like to be here. "And how do I know it wasn't you and you're trying to trip me up?"

Sage leaned back. "I was only ten when she was killed. I don't remember you or Abby. Sorry."

Kirk didn't hold that against him. "I'm thirty-five." He'd been aware of the younger Madison because he'd seen him in town. Around the time of Abby's murder there'd been more of them, younger and older. "Do you remember anything from the gathering back then?"

Around them other people were talking about TV shows, their co-workers, or kids. Sage and Kirk were talking murder.

Sage shook his head. "It wouldn't be anyone under your age, for the simple reason the shifting doesn't kick in until late puberty, sixteen to eighteen. The last years of high school are the worst. Hormones, homework, and hair. That's the first thing, waking up furry. It brushes off in daylight, but within the next month..." He shook his head as though the memories were best left untouched.

Kirk's magic had hit around the same time. While other kids were struggling with acne and trying to get a date, the paranormal kids were trying to work out how to live in a world that didn't want them to exist. "So, the killer is over thirty-five." Probably older, but how much older? "Who was here then and now?"

"I couldn't tell you. I might be able to recognize the scent if you had something."

Kirk shook his head and touched his neck. "He bit her."

"That's what we do. It's quick, if that's any consolation." Sage sounded sincere. And it did mean something to know she hadn't suffered.

The waitress stepped up to the table and topped off their wine glasses. "Can I take your plates? Would you like a dessert menu?"

"No." Kirk said a bit too fast.

"Yes," Sage said with a smile like he was innocent of all charges even while blood dripped off his fingers.

I don't need this distraction.

But Sage was pretty, in that strong jawed, blue eyed way. He was far too clean cut. What would it be like to run his fingers through his pelt? That would be safe as they wouldn't be skin to skin. That he was craving even that small amount of contact was a sad statement about Kirk's life. Maybe he needed to get a pet.

The waitress looked at Kirk. "Coffee?"

"Sure." If Sage was getting dessert he might as well sit there. It was the closest thing he'd had to a date...ever. "Black."

The waitress moved on to the next table.

Sage leaned forward. "You don't have to rush. You can still enjoy dinner out."

"I can't. My diet raises questions." And then one thing would lead to another and he really couldn't deal with having another would be lover pass out.

"Others like us wouldn't mind."

"Others like you tend to kill others like me."

Sage frowned. "I haven't heard that before."

"You haven't met any like me before."

Sage selected a fancy chocolate tart for dessert. It looked amazing when it arrived. His own coffee was rather dull in comparison even though it came with a chocolate on the side.

"This is really good." Sage made a small groan of appreciation and Kirk assumed he'd done it very deliberately.

"Torture me why don't you." He sipped his coffee and pretended that he didn't like food, that he only ate it because his body still required some.

Sage smiled. "I don't usually share desserts, but you can have a bite."

"I don't want a bite." He didn't need or want anything that Sage was offering.

"I can see that you do. Your eyes color shifts. I've never seen eyes that color. More amber than brown." He scooped up a spoonful of tart and held it out.

It would be churlish to refuse; however, he didn't want to give into the cat. He hesitated, and Sage lifted an eyebrow. Kirk was trapped by his own desire. Damn.

He accepted the spoon without touching Sage. The tart was amazing, silky and just the right amount of bitter with shards of toffee on top. Maybe he should've skipped the steak and gone straight to dessert. "Thank you."

He handed the spoon back and Sage ran his fingers over the back of Kirk's hand like he couldn't help but touch him.

"Was it a male?"

Kirk blinked and realized they were back to talking suspects. "Yes. I heard them arguing, but by the time I got there all I saw was the attack. I hid. I didn't want to be next." He glanced away. "I should've done something."

"With what? Your bare hands? I grew up around them and

I wouldn't go anywhere near a pissed off cougar." He said it a little too loud a couple of people glanced over.

There were too many people around and they were drawing too much attention—even if people weren't trying to listen in to their conversation. "We should leave."

"Your place or mine." Sage grinned.

Kirk glared at him. This was business, not pleasure. And he doubted that showing up at the ranch as Sage's hook up would go down well.

Sage considered him for a moment. "Right, your place."

"That's..." He sighed. No one's place was what he'd been thinking. He didn't want Sage in his room. He'd make it smell like cinnamon and sex and Kirk would never get control of the need to touch and be touched. He hadn't been this aroused with another since his twenty-first birthday.

It was going to end up much the same. Him alone with a box of tissues.

———

SAGE KNEW he shouldn't want to touch Kirk. Every time their skin connected shivers of electricity slid down his back in the nicest possible way. He knew what he was feeling was little bits of his energy and life being taken by Kirk, but honestly, he'd never felt better.

He left his truck in the restaurant car park and walked to the B&B with Kirk. They slipped inside like thieves, like they were going to do more than talk. If sex were on the table, Sage would've agreed in less than a heartbeat. He'd noticed the way Kirk had tucked the notebook into his jacket pocket and readjusted his jeans before he'd paid the bill for both of them as though they had been on a date. Sage had been on worse, and much weirder, dates.

This wasn't even top ten on either scale.

Despite the talk of murder.

Really, dinner with a vampire should rate in his top ten weird dates, but that was the hazard of being a paranormal. There was no such thing as normal dates; there was always something to complicate things. But tonight, he was having fun, and Kirk was serious and trying to be proper and keep his distance which only made Sage want to keep brushing up against him to see how far things would go. To see how much Kirk would take. When would he feel the loss of life?

Sage didn't even like people touching him most of the time. But he struggled to keep his hands off of Kirk. He let the back of his hand brush against Kirk's again.

Kirk pulled away. "You are determined to die tonight, aren't you?"

"You won't kill me." Not tonight at least. He'd seen the way Kirk looked at him when he thought Sage wasn't paying attention and it was very similar to the way Kirk looked at the steak he couldn't eat.

Kirk gave him a look that clearly said *try me.* "Just keep your voice down."

"Aren't you the only person here?"

"I think so. But still, it's polite and I don't want the owner hearing."

Sage sat on the bed and gave a bounce. It didn't squeak unfortunately. "What's in the notebook?"

"Nothing."

So, something.

The silence grew between them. Sage resisted the urge to pounce and pull Kirk in for the kiss the way he wanted. That's what should have happened next. Or Kirk should be pressing him to the bed and scrambling to get his clothes off.

Sage glanced down. He was here to help catch a killer not get lucky. "Do you have pen and paper?"

"Why?" The wariness was back.

"So, I can draw my family tree and we can limit the suspects to men over thirty-five." He'd already drawn up a list in his head, but maybe he was forgetting someone. Maybe someone who attended twenty years ago, and not again. "You should talk to the seer."

"Who?"

"Seer. She can see futures, but she also knows all the family tree stuff." She'd have access to more detailed records, which would better than his memory.

Kirk's eyebrows pinched together. "What's in your future?"

"Trouble...that you bring."

"I told you I was bad news."

"That's not what she said. I have to help you because trouble is coming, and I can prevent it or lessen it." He paused; Violet hadn't been very clear on the details. "Maybe the killer discovers you're here."

"That means he's at the gathering." Kirk opened the notebook to a blank page and handed it over. So, who is here and over thirty-five?"

Sage drew two columns. One for people that were here, and one for people that weren't. There were seven names on the here side and another twelve on the other. He'd probably missed some, too. "It's too many names. You're going to need to give me something more."

"Who was into eighteen-year-old girls?"

Sage wrinkled his nose. "Was it a date gone bad?"

"I don't know. I didn't want to know who she was doing in her spare time."

"I want to cross my brothers off. They wouldn't." And he was holding on to that belief.

"It wasn't Stone. I knew him from school, so I would've recognized his energy if not his cougar form."

Relief swept through him as Sage crossed of the name. The thought that had been nagging him finally became clear. "Wait...how did you know it was one of us? Did you know we were shifters back then?" Something in Kirk's story didn't add up. "You didn't see the shift? Where were the clothes?"

It took more than a few seconds to shift, and while shifting they were vulnerable.

"I didn't know you were shifters, but Mom warned me and Abby about you lot and to stay away. I don't know why. I guess this had started to kick in around then because I could feel the difference between a shifter and a human—not that I used those words back then because I didn't know shifters were a thing. Maybe Madison and human would be better. You vibrate differently, and it feels rawer. Human energy is..." He cupped his hands. "Smooth is the only way I can describe it."

"So even with your eyes closed you can tell who is human and who isn't?"

"Yeah. I can track you now; I've tasted your life."

That was both exhilarating and troubling, even though Sage could do the same by scent. While he was used to his family being able to track him, he wasn't used to it from others. "And you're sure you could pick the killer out of a crowd?"

"Yes. I didn't touch him, but I'll never forget the way his energy felt as he killed her. It was like being dropped in an ice bath and drowning. That was the day this magic really kicked in. Before that I could ignore it, pretend nothing was happing even though there was something wrong with me."

"There's nothing wrong with you. You just weren't told what you were."

Kirk flexed his hands and leaned against the wall. "Being

told wouldn't have changed anything. And I couldn't have saved her."

"So you heard an argument, but what you saw was a cougar. Where was this?"

"Behind the video store, now cupcake shop."

"But she wasn't found there."

"No, she was found at the river, just like Mom."

Kirk's story matched what Davy Greenwood had told Sage. Davy was suspicious because her neck had been sliced open, but it was brushed off as an after-death animal attack.

"That means whoever did it had to shift twice and then take her to the river." That wasn't something that a teen in their first few years of shifting could pull off. "How long did you watch for?"

"I was hiding. When the cat stalked away, I ran. I didn't stop to check on her, I didn't call for help, I fled. I knew it was one of you lot and not a wild animal because I could feel it. The same way I could feel she was dead. Her life petered out to nothing as I sat there paralyzed by fear."

Sage got off the bed and crossed the room to where Kirk stood by the empty fireplace, his fists clenched by his side. Sage put his hands on Kirk's shirt clad upper arms. There was no spark between them this time. "Most people would've hidden."

"I know, but maybe he would've run off if I'd done something."

"Or maybe he would've hunted you down. You need to forgive yourself for hiding. You were a kid. A kid with a weird power you didn't know how to explain." Sage didn't know what he would've done if he had no one to tell him what was happening when the world had smelled sharper. Or when he'd woken up human but covered in fur. He pulled Kirk into an embrace, expecting to feel that now familiar buzz. "I'm not feeling the static on your skin."

"Because our skin isn't touching." Kirk carefully rested his cheek on Sage's shoulder instead of pulling away.

Well, didn't that open up a whole world of possibilities?

He was not thinking about any of them. Firstly, there was a murder to solve. Secondly, Kirk was a vampire and apparently other paranormals hunted them and there had to be a reason for that.

But on the other hand, he smelled good and there was something about him that Sage couldn't quite resist—beside his amber eyes and his seriousness and the way he'd come back to make things right for his sister. Here was a guy who'd managed to survive being paranormal on his own. Sage had never known a day without his family.

He'd crumble by himself, but Kirk had come out stronger.

Kirk wasn't the kind of guy Sage usually met, either online or when he went out looking for company. Sage wanted to turn his head and kiss Kirk just to feel the current run beneath his skin. If he did that though, Kirk would pull away. He'd put up the barrier and they'd talk about death and nothing more.

But they should be talking about life. Kirk made him feel like it was spring, and the world was waking and full of possibilities before settling into the slower, more syrupy pace of summer. It wasn't cold dead earth that Kirk smelled like, but the kind that gave rise to forests.

Though at the moment, there was only one tree that was getting a rise. Dinner had been enough for him to start thinking about what might happen after. He wanted to get Kirk naked. Taste his skin and inhale his scent after he came.

Kirk's arms went around his waist, and Sage risked leaning closer. He pressed against Kirk, so they were hip to hip. And was happy to realize the desire wasn't his alone; Kirk was just as hard with expectation. For several heart beats, he didn't know if he should just enjoy the moment or press for more. His hunger won out.

Sage rolled his hips. "I've got an idea."

"I don't like your ideas." Kirk started to pull away. "We can't do this."

"We can. With our clothes on, no skin touching." The words tumbled out fast. He kept hold of Kirk, not wanting to lose the contact.

Kirk stared up at him, no lust in his gaze. Only worry. "The last person I was with passed out."

"I know the risk, and we'll both be careful." He wanted Kirk more than anything. A need hummed in Sage's blood like a hundred bees seeking escape.

Kirk's eyes glowed in the softly lit room. It would be easy to slip and fall and drown in the whisky amber. His lips parted, and Sage was sure he was about to say no so Sage rushed on to try and salvage the mess.

"If you really don't want to try, tell me to leave. I'll still help. But when I'm around you..."

He licked his lip. Sage didn't know what it was but from the moment he'd seen Kirk in the diner there'd been something. It was the kind of spark that shouldn't be ignored in case it accidentally started a wildfire.

"Stay."

CHAPTER SEVEN

IT WAS the stupid thing to say, but no other word would form. He wanted Sage, and not in the need to eat way. He needed him naked and in bed. It had been over a decade since he'd been so consumed with lust that he let himself wander so dangerously close with another. Maybe that was all this was, simple lust because Sage knew what he was, and Kirk didn't have to pretend. He could tell Sage not to touch his skin and they would both be safe. But nothing about this felt safe.

That Sage was tall, blue eyed and a little too confident were all things he'd once hated, but since leaving Madison Gully he'd admired in others. He'd fallen for more than one guy like this before pushing them away. What the hell was wrong with him?

Sage pressed him against the wall in two smooth steps. His hands bracketed Kirk's head and his hips pressed close, leaving no doubt. He'd felt the change in Sage's energy, the subtle ramping up, the sweetening. Now he knew what it was, Sage's desire was unmistakable.

"I want to kiss you," Sage murmured.

"We agreed no skin." It had been years. Maybe he had

better control and he wouldn't hurt Sage, but he didn't want to risk it either. What if they became too caught up in the moment?

"Okay." But Sage didn't sound convinced and Kirk's resolve weakened.

Sage had nice lips, the kind that should be kissed. He didn't even know the name of the last person to kiss him it had been so long ago. "This isn't a pity fuck."

Sage rolled his hips. "No...unless you feel sad for me, stuck in the Gully."

Kirk smiled, and gripped Sage's hips so he could move against the hard length in the shifter's jeans. "Pretty sure you've got more experience with dates and sex than me."

"Maybe, but this is a first."

He'd never gotten this close to a shifter before; this was new for both of them. They should both know better, but the lust demanded to be explored. It scoured his veins with hot need.

Sage moved closer so there was no gap between them and inhaled deeply. "I like the way you smell." He glanced away. "That too weird? I wouldn't usually say anything but given were both—"

"It's not weird. I like the way your energy feels and tastes. Like cinnamon and musk...a fresh cookie." He wanted to touch and to taste but couldn't allow himself that pleasure.

"You're a forest I want to run in." Sage's breath was on his ear. If either of them turned their head there'd be accidental contact.

Sage ground his hips against Kirk as he rutted against him. It would be easy to shove his hands beneath Sage's shirt, run his hands over his skin and then slide lower, undo his belt and push down his jeans so he could take that hard length in his hands... his mouth.

He closed his eyes. The press of the wall at his back and the heat of Sage against his front...it was almost enough.

"How many layers of clothing do we need?"

"No skin contact." They needed to keep their jeans and long sleeves on. Maybe this wasn't going to work...but he wanted it to. For the first time in too long he had the chance to be with someone even if it was in a limited fashion.

Sage's desire pressed against his own, and he pushed Sage away. Sage bit back a groan. "I need..."

"Put your hands on the wall." Sage's eyebrows knitted for a moment then he did, as though the position was too familiar. Kirk encircled Sage's waist with his arm and ground against the curve of his ass. "Is this what you like?"

"Yeah. How?"

"Lucky guess." He trailed his hand over the ridge in Sage's jeans, cupped his balls then stroked upward. "I would love to sink into you. Every stroke you'd feel that tingle down your spine as I tasted you."

Sage's breath hitched.

Kirk kept going. He was close.

"Touch me. Please."

He didn't want to, but he needed to. If he did, this would be over. He pressed his lips to the back of Sages neck, keeping the hunger locked down. But it was still there, the taste of cinnamon and the frisson of energy. Sage groaned, working himself in Kirk's hand.

The energy shifted, sweet like honey as Sage came.

Kirk gave in, wishing he was buried balls deep in Sage's ass.

He rested his forehead on Sage's shoulder. No more skin contact. Their breathing was hard, and Kirk wasn't sure he trusted himself to stand on his own. It had been too long since he'd had a lover.

Whatever this had been, he wanted to do it again. Maybe there was a way...

He let his hands fall away from Sage and stepped back. There was a box of tissues on the mantelpiece and he offered them to Sage.

"I might go to the bathroom."

"Sure. It's at the end of the hall."

Sage gave Kirk a small smile and slipped away. Then Kirk was alone in his room. He pulled out a handful of tissues, cleaned up the best he could before realizing when Sage left, he'd need a shower before bed anyway. His skin smelled of the shifter and as nice as it was, he'd never get any sleep. He'd just relive this moment again and again wanting more.

He shouldn't have let it happen. He'd spent years building up walls to protect himself and others. Sage had brought them down with a smile and a touch.

What had they been talking about before? How had that ended up happening? He wasn't sure, but he wouldn't take it back or push Sage away. But even as his thoughts spiraled out reaching for new possibilities, he reined them back to dull reality.

He was here to find a killer, not a lover.

The door opened and Sage stepped back in. His energy was jittery as though *he'd* fed.

"Are you okay?"

"Yeah." Sage grinned. "I didn't actually think anything would happen..." That made two of them. "Next time something thinner than jeans would be nice."

Next time. As much as Kirk wanted a next time, they shouldn't. How long until one of them screwed up? "Maybe we should focus for a bit."

Hurt shimmered in Sage's eyes, then he blinked and looked away. "Sure."

"I don't want to rush and hurt you." Kirk cracked his knuckles. Now that lust had been sated, the hunger was rising, and Sage tasted so good. He shouldn't be hungry, but he couldn't tamp it down.

He could see the argument form as Sage opened his mouth, then he nodded and the hurt and heat were gone. His energy calmed and a nonphysical distance formed. "You're right."

Sage ran his hand over his hair and glanced around the room as though looking for something safe to discuss. Or was he trying to find an excuse to leave? Was he realizing the dangerous game he was playing with a vampire? Were regrets now rising?

There would be no next time. In daylight Sage would see this for what it was—rash and foolish. Vampires didn't get to have families.

His mother had tried and failed.

His mentor had eventually been driven mad by the need to feed and a hunger for more power. That would be his fate, too. Maybe he should follow the family tradition of ending up at the river.

Sage picked up the brochures. "Sightseeing or spying?"

"I thought about staying at the ranch...but you had no vacancies."

He pressed his lips together. "That wouldn't be safe. You said you knew the killer from his energy, that it was a Madison. What did he feel like?"

"I felt a cold rush, like I was drowning in a winter frost rimmed river, but it wasn't sharp. The energy was smooth like a river stone and left a taste like gin." He only knew that because he'd stolen some of his mother's liquor. But that memory was old; what if it was wrong, and he'd built it up to be something that it wasn't? Maybe it had been his own fear swamping him. "Remind you of anyone?"

Sage shook his head. "Your descriptions aren't how I smell things."

"How do you smell?"

"Like...I don't know. How would you describe your energy?"

"Like a cactus trying to push through my skin at times. A pulse."

Sage shook his head. "It's earth and metal and wildness that calls to me. It's weird." He shrugged. "Maybe that's normal for vampires."

"My mentor was like an old house. Eventually he smelled like rotting wood and decay." The overwhelming scent of death had become disconcerting and Kirk had investigated. The truth had been revolting. "My mother...I was too young to know. But I remember her like a moth. When my father's light went out, she couldn't go on."

"She killed him."

"Not intentionally." But intentions didn't matter when a touch stole the life you wanted to protect at all cost.

Sage flapped the brochure. "If you want to go riding near the ranch, I'll take you, but if you can recognize the killer from their energy, they might be able to recognize you by scent. That's my cell phone on the brochure. Don't lose it." He smiled and stepped closer, not to kiss him, but to give him a quick and safe embrace. "I want to do this again."

———

SAGE TAPPED the steering wheel as he drove home. He was smiling when he shouldn't be. While he'd doubted Kirk at first and had been concerned about the implication, Sage was now sure one of his family was a killer. Not only that but the killer had shifted in town, risking exposing the whole family.

But all he wanted to think about was the way Kirk had felt against him, the way his body had moved and the way he didn't want to touch him and hurt him.

He rubbed the back of his neck where Kirk's lips had touched, sure he could still feel the static on his skin. He shivered, and lust tumbled through him, rough and ready to rise again. He had to get himself together before he parked. As he turned into the driveway, he wasn't sure he could.

Whoever ran into him would smell Kirk on his skin. Well, they'd smell a man and sex. He was sure he wouldn't get away with it without being quizzed.

And he had no idea what he was going to say. To them it would look like he'd blown off the family barbeque to be with his boyfriend. Maybe all he needed to do was agree. It wouldn't be the first time someone hadn't come for the gathering because they were in a new relationship or they had other plans. It wasn't compulsory. Nor was the ranch closed to family the rest of the time. But this was the big event.

Just because he lived here, didn't mean he couldn't have a life beyond the ranch.

He pulled up; his spot still taken by the red sports car. Next time he was going to put up a sign that said *for ranch vehicles only*. He didn't have to open the truck door to hear the music. The party was still going. For several seconds he deliberated on grabbing a beer and joining in, but he'd much rather have a shower and go to bed without speaking to anyone. He didn't want others to ruin the night or the memory. It was his to enjoy. Come morning he'd have to think about who might taste like frost and gin.

He got out and went to the main house. The kitchen light was on, but he made straight for the stairs, hoping to avoid whoever was up.

"That you Sage?"

He winced at Stone's voice. Had his brother been waiting for him to get home? Sage considered ignoring him but decided better of it. He strode to the kitchen where Stone was at the kitchen table nursing a coffee. Clay sat next to him.

He was clearly in the shit and he didn't know what he'd done.

Clay sniffed, his gaze skimming over him as though he knew exactly where he'd been but was going to proceed with the interview to get a full confession. "You weren't at the barbeque."

Sage shoved his hands into his pockets. "I had other places to be."

"It's the gathering," Stone said.

"I know. Kind of hard to miss." His home was filled with people, some of whom didn't care about the everyday running of the ranch and business. To them the gathering was nothing more than a free holiday.

"Don't be smart. Where have you been?" Clay pressed. His eyes more grey than blue. Like rocks.

Sage lifted his gaze to meet his brother's. "None of your business. I'm not a kid."

Stone's lips curved. "You *are* seeing someone."

Sage deliberated for a moment. He wasn't really seeing anyone, but would the lie make his life easier or more complicated? "And?"

Clay shook his head. "You couldn't put it on hold for another week?"

"Why should I have to? There's plenty of hands to help out. Why can't I have a break?" The words were out of his mouth before he had a chance to think about the consequences.

Clay opened his mouth, but Stone put a hand on his older brother's arm. "Is that all it is? You just want to have a break? Or do you want to leave?"

Sage chewed over the question for several heartbeats. He could leave. He wasn't a Madison, but this was his home. "I love it here. But I would like a week off sometimes. Mom would, too."

Clay brushed off Stone's hand. "How long have you felt like this?"

It wasn't just because of Kirk. He'd been wanting something for a while, he'd just never been brave enough to face it and pin it down. "A few years."

"Sage...why didn't you call us?" Stone looked genuinely concerned.

"Because you have a life elsewhere. I need to make this work." He didn't know how to have the ranch and a life and a partner. Kirk would go back to the city and then what? They might keep it going for a few months but then Kirk would get bored, or Sage would want more. They couldn't even touch properly.

He sighed. He shouldn't be thinking it was anything more than convenience. Two gay paranormals in a small town...of course something was going to happen.

But Kirk had tried to make sure it wouldn't.

"And part of that is saying get your ass down here so I can have a holiday," Stone said.

Sage shrugged. "Maybe. Can we do this in the morning?"

"Sit," Clay said. "Do you want coffee?"

"Am I going to need it?" Sage pulled out a chair and sat, wishing he'd ignored Stone and gone to bed. Would they have followed him up and accosted him in the hallway? When his brothers wanted something, they were persistent.

"No, we were worried about you...but now we know you're fine. How's Mom. Really?"

"She's..." He glanced at his brothers, knowing they deserved the truth. "She doesn't go for runs anymore, but she'll shift and sit in the moonlight. She wants to go and see her sister; I said I'd manage while she's away." He didn't think she was ready to find a quiet spot for her last shift. She was too young to die. "She's only sixty-five."

But she did all the books and a lot of the scheduling while Sage did all the manual labor. He was learning the other bits, but there were only so many hours in a day. When the three of them were kids she must have leaned heavily on Clay and Stone to help around the ranch, as well as hiring help. Is that why his brothers had left as soon as they could?

Stone nodded. "You think if we come down for a week to take over things, that will be enough?"

"Why don't you ask her?"

Clay lifted one blond eyebrow. "Because it will take us twice as long to get it out of her. We had to ambush you."

They'd waited until he was tired and thinking of other things. "Is that all?"

"We worry. She's not getting younger and you're...you're here alone," Stone said carefully.

"Well then maybe don't jump down my throat when I do get a chance to see someone." He shoved back his chair. "It's new so don't be yapping okay?"

By new he meant it wasn't going to last. He'd just make the most of it while he could.

"Sure," Clay said getting up. "You going to be around tomorrow?"

"I'm going to take a couple of horses out." Hopefully Kirk wouldn't change his mind. He didn't care if he missed the rest of the gathering. The seer had told him to help Kirk and he was. If his brothers thought he was dating, why couldn't it be both?

"So that's a no."

"Yeah." He was going to do whatever he wanted and let his

brothers pick up the slack. If they grumbled, he wouldn't be able to trust them if he took a week off and went somewhere, like to the city to see Kirk. He didn't even know what Kirk did or where he lived or what hobbies he had.

"Just be careful. Some people aren't happy with the way things are." Clay gave Sage's shoulder a squeeze as he walked past, interview over.

The warning meant Mica and Ash were stirring up dissent. Were they reminding anyone who would listen that Sage didn't belong on the ranch? The seer thought Mom and Sage were safe but if the others pooled their money and a case was made, they could be forced to sell. As much as he wanted some time off, leaving forever would kill him. This was his home and his life.

Maybe the seer had seen this trouble and the danger to the ranch.

"He got a name?" Stone whispered after Clay left.

Sage considered his brother. "Yeah, you might know him."

"How so?"

"You went to school with him." He watched as Stone thought back to high school. "Kirk Gracewell."

Stone mouthed the name. "Was that the kid whose mother and sister killed themselves?"

Sage nodded carefully, not willing to reveal the truth about Abby's death. "What do you remember about him?"

"Not much. Our cousins didn't like him or his sister. They had an issue with the family."

"What issue?"

"I don't know. Kid stuff. Maybe the sister knocked them back." He smiled. "She was pretty but also scary if you know what I mean. Guys either worshipped her from afar or they teased her. But even then, I think they were scared of her."

"So, you liked her."

"She was a few years older, in Clay's year, I think. You didn't want to say anything in front of him."

He liked Clay, but the age gap between them meant that he didn't really know him. Sage hadn't even been in high school when Clay had gone to college. Sage shrugged. "I wanted to know more about Kirk, not Abby."

"All I remember is a quiet kid who aced science and sport. He was good with his hands." He smiled. "Guess some things haven't changed."

That was truer than Stone realized.

CHAPTER EIGHT

SAGE DIDN'T LINGER in bed, even though he wanted to. He didn't want to face the questions or explain his absences. But he needed to put in an appearance and, more importantly, make sure the animals were being looked after.

Kids raced around the house, as though this was the first time they'd been let loose. A few adults were up, and he nodded to them as he went by. They clutched their coffee and remained bundled up against the early morning chill. Others wouldn't rise until lunch time when they'd caught up on sleep and slept off the hangover.

Sage had always liked the way the cold air cut through his lungs and scoured him clean. This morning was no different. He'd slept without hearing the tail end of the barbeque, wrapped up in dreams of things that couldn't happen. He'd woken with a peculiar desire that seemed to have been fed overnight and left him both hungry and sated and totally confused.

A text message this morning had put a smile on his face that couldn't be wiped off.

Kirk still wanted to go horse riding, though he'd confessed to never doing it before. That would be fine. They could just amble along the trails. Take some time to talk about something other than Abby.

And not take their clothes off.

There had to be another way.

He was as light as a feather as he made his way to the stable. It was a ridiculous notion, and an equally stupid way to feel. He barely knew Kirk but even the idea of seeing him made him want to bounce.

"You look pretty happy with yourself." Ash leaned on the fence near the alpaca water trough.

"Yep. It's a lovely day and I'm going riding."

Ash cut him a glare. "You're supposed to be spending time with your family. Guess it doesn't matter."

Sage's mood fractured, but he didn't want his damn cousin getting to him. "You got a problem with me working? Taking *paying* clients riding? The ranch doesn't come to a standstill just because family turned up."

"Client...is that what you call it? The way I hear it, you've been sniffing around a tourist in town."

"Maybe the tourist is here because of me."

"Why not tell him to wait until we leave?"

"Because this is when he could take time off. If he wants to ride and fish and do other ranch activities while he's here, then I'm going to take him. I don't need to justify my life to you." He just had though, and it irked him. But if he'd said nothing Ash would think he was lying. He probably did anyway.

Ash nodded. "So, anyone can go riding?"

"Not this morning; it's a private booking. But if you want to go out this afternoon, I'm happy to head out again. Just let Mom know and she'll put it in my schedule."

"I might do that."

"Great. I'm sure some of the older kids would like it, too." He turned and walked away before Ash could get deeper under his skin.

That Ash knew he'd been meeting up with someone in town troubled him. Was Ash watching him or had it been gossip? Either way he needed to be careful. But careful of what? How could he avoid Kirk when they needed to work together—and more importantly when Sage didn't want to avoid him. He wanted to spend his free time with Kirk and not just because the seer told him that he had to.

Maybe Ash was just pissy because he had to help with the chores. It seemed no one wanted him to do his own thing. They'd much rather him be here, all the time, at their beck and call and doing all the work so they could relax.

He saddled two horses and walked them across the yard, tying them up by the house—something he wouldn't usually bother with but all the shifters around was making them a bit skittish. He knew how they felt, even though he'd been raised around them. The scent of so many cougars made him jumpy.

In the house he grabbed the picnic lunch he'd put together and some bottles of water. He wrote on the board where he'd be—a system that had been in place long before he'd come along. No one went out on the property without leaving a note about where they were going and what they were travelling on. Horse, truck, 4...as in their own four legs.

A few minutes later he was riding to the nearest trail to meet Kirk at the bridge.

———

KIRK HAD GOTTEN a lift to the bridge with the lady who ran

the B&B. He could've taken his bike but leaving it in such a quiet spot would invite trouble. Or maybe he was thinking like a city dweller. Twenty years ago, he'd have pinched everything on the bike that wasn't glued on. The compartments, while secure, could be unscrewed, taken away and broken into at leisure. Now he waited, hands shoved in his pockets against the chill and the air as sharp as a knife on his tongue. Overhead orange leaves rustled, occasionally drifting to the ground.

The world here was alive in a way that the city never was. In the city he was never far from a fresh burst of power, a new taste. A million different meals to sample as he brushed by. Here there was energy all around him. Pulsing and tempting. Kirk could feel it, but he couldn't taste it or use it. He'd starve in the wilderness. It was like standing on the street staring into the diner, smelling the pies and chips, but unable to eat anything.

But this morning he wasn't hungry. There was only one person he wanted to taste and that troubled him. He shouldn't crave just one person when the world was a smorgasbord of delights with just the occasional rancid tidbit.

The river ran smooth and fast and if he followed it, it would curve around to the park and the foot bridge where he'd been yesterday. A little further on would be where his sister was found.

The hair on the back of his neck prickled as though he was being watched. He didn't turn, though; instead he closed his eyes and reached out with his mind. There was something there. He breathed in and flexed his fingers on the railing. His knuckles cracked. He brushed against the energy and the image sharpened. There was a cougar about twenty yards away in the shadows.

He felt the claws, but also the human. True animals had a very different energy to shifters. He couldn't feed off animals, but shifters were fair game. The watching cougar wasn't Sage.

This one was heavy like lead on his tongue, paprika and honey. He didn't know who it was. Which meant he hadn't gone to school with them.

But it wasn't Abby's killer either.

Three new lives caught his attention. The throbbing steady heat of two big animals and Sage. He knew it was Sage. Having tasted him he could sense him at a distance. Kirk's heart gave a very disconcerting bounce of anticipation.

The cougar in the trees slunk away.

Kirk opened his eyes and stretched. He couldn't see any of them yet. It was another two minutes before Sage appeared on the trail riding one horse and towing the other, though it probably wasn't called towing when it came to horses.

They were awfully big.

When he'd woken up hard and full of enthusiasm to see Sage again, this had seemed like a really fun idea. They would be alone on the trail and he'd let himself imagine all kinds of things. Several tissues later after he'd given into lust, he'd texted Sage.

His mentor had always said not to be led by the heart. And he'd seen the damage love had done to both his parents. But he wasn't in love; he was just enjoying having some kind of sex life for the first time in far too long.

Maybe there were other vampires who knew how to have a life. He needed to find them, ask someone how he was supposed to deal with the loss of food and touch. While he couldn't change what he was, he didn't want to be a lonely recluse only venturing out to taste life when he was starving.

"Been waiting long?"

"Not really. I was enjoying the morning." Neither of which were a lie. He gazed up at Sage.

The horse blew out a breath that made its lips flap. They didn't eat people, but they could still bite. They could crush someone with their weight. Break a foot. He was sure he'd smell like fear and he didn't like it. Most people feared him; he was a vampire.

The horses didn't seem to care.

Sage tilted his head and sniffed the air. His eyes narrowed for a split second and his voice was low when he spoke. "Did you see anyone?"

"There was a cougar hiding in the shadows." Kirk tilted his head but didn't point in case they were still watching. "I didn't recognize them."

"My brother, Clay." Sage smiled and shook his head. "They just can't let me do my own thing."

"I can cross him off the list." Kirk smiled, but it was as fragile as the frost edging the river.

Sage sighed and nodded. "Yes." He swung his leg off the horse and landed neatly on the ground. "Because you weren't sure, this is the front." He gave the horse a scratch around the ears. "If you go around the back, stay out of kicking distance. They shouldn't, but you never know."

"This seemed like a really good idea this morning."

"It'll be fine. This dappled fellow is Donut; he's a total plodder who's more interested in eating flowers than moving at any speed."

He'd been given the horse equivalent of a tricycle and that suited him fine. "How do I get up there?"

"Foot in the stirrup then pull up and swing over. I can give you a boost if you need it."

Sage was already giving him a lift. Just being around him made the world brighter. And once he'd found Abby's killer, there'd be nothing but murder between them. Kirk would go back to the city and this would become nothing more than a memory of the things he couldn't have. Even the thought ached like an old wound that wouldn't heal.

Maybe there'd be another shifter willing to look past what he was. But in the city they were more likely to report him to the Coven. That was one of the reasons his mentor had hunted among the street kids; no one would miss them and there'd be one less shifter to sniff out the vampires. It was no wonder his mentor had feared the Coven since he'd hunted and killed so many always searching for the one shifter who'd increase his power.

Kirk had thought it a myth...now he wasn't so sure. When he was with Sage everything felt different. But he didn't want to destroy him, and that was all that would happen. Kirk would end up bleeding him dry.

That wouldn't stop him from making the most of the time they had, though.

The horse huffed at him and Kirk stepped back. A motorbike seemed so much safer. "And when Donut throws me off and I land on my ass?"

"I'll be very polite and not laugh at you." But Sage was grinning like this was all very amusing.

"Tomorrow I should take you riding my style."

"On your bike?"

"Yeah. Or do you not like things without four legs or four wheels?"

Sage's smile became a little more rigid. "You'll be fine."

And just like that they were spending tomorrow together. It was too easy being with Sage. Far easier than getting up on Donut who deliberately took a step as Kirk tried to get on. Sage held Donut a bit more firmly. Kirk put his hand on the horse to steady himself before pulling up. Donut was hot like slow flowing lava.

"Are you eating Donut?"

"No. I was trying to feel the energy to see if I could..." He shrugged. He wasn't a nature witch. He had no control over animals or plants and couldn't use their energy either—that would've made life so much easier. The only beings he could control were humans. He could grab their energy, feed, and make them bend to his will. His mentor had done it all the time like it was a game. That was how he'd learned. He rarely did it now because it didn't feel right to manipulate others.

He swung up onto Donut. Donut flicked his ears and glanced at him; Kirk was almost sure the horse was laughing at him.

Sage put a hand on Kirk's leg and gave him the reins. "That wasn't so bad."

With the denim between them the touch was safe. He'd gone without touch for so long, the fear of taking too much or having someone touch him easily and willingly was unsettling. That he craved it was dangerous.

He couldn't fall into the very pretty trap that was Sage.

———

SAGE COULDN'T HELP but be alert for his brother spying on him. Irritation bristled beneath his skin. He wasn't a cub in need of supervision, and he could take care of himself. That Clay had taken it upon himself to follow Kirk annoyed Sage, but that Clay knew who Sage was seeing meant that Stone had open his big mouth.

Was nothing private? Now the two of them knew...how long until everyone knew he was helping Kirk hunt a killer?

"You're scowling about something." Kirk broke into his thoughts.

Sage shook his head to scatter them. "Yeah, and I shouldn't be. It's a beautiful day." And he was riding next to the man he wanted to do more than rub up against. The whisky of Kirk's eyes was brighter on the trail; the orange leaves and shadows suited him. As though he belonged out here. He smiled, but he couldn't bitch about his family when Kirk had none. He had no doubt Kirk would've done anything to have his sister alive to gripe about. "How's your ass travelling?"

"What ass? I think it went numb about half an hour ago."

"You've only been riding half an hour."

"And?" Kirk lifted an eyebrow.

Sage smiled and relaxed. Let Clay stalk them; there was no crime to enjoy a winter ride with an attractive man. It would be a crime not to. "So, what do you in the city?"

Kirk glanced at him. "Why?"

"I want to get to know..." He bit off the last word. Was Kirk not thinking of more?

He was silent for several seconds. "I'm a hospital orderly."

"Do you get away much?"

"There was no need for me to go anywhere...and where would I go? What would I do? How often do you get away?"

Sage licked his lower lip. Not enough and yet at the same time he didn't want to leave. "I go into the city about once a month, just for a night. Maybe two if we're quiet."

"Then you're doing better than me." The silence settled again, like a blanket they could share and keep warm beneath. "But I like the idea of taking time off." He smiled at Sage.

Sage tried not to get too hopeful. "I'm negotiating to get a week off, but it means one of my brothers will have to come down. Not much of a holiday for them."

"Is this your break, while you have plenty of hands?"

Sage laughed. "The help isn't willing." The silence breathed between them. The forest was never quiet, but they were alone, and they didn't have to talk about the murder. He wanted to learn more about Kirk and what his life had been like. "So, what did you do when you left town?"

"I slept in parks and under bridges."

Sage snapped his head around to stare at Kirk. "But you'd have only been fifteen."

He shrugged, swaying in time with Donut's steps. "There wasn't much else I could do. Eventually I fell in with some other paranormal kids. I tried to keep what I could do hidden because I didn't want them to force me out. After about six months or so a man came to us. He knew what I was just by looking at me, and I could feel it in him. He taught me how to hide and survive."

"And he was the one that told you vampires are hunted."

"Yeah. Besides Mom, he was the only one I'd ever met. Mom didn't have these marks. I don't think she knew."

"Have you heard of the Coven?"

"Are you going to report me?" Fear edged Kirk's voice.

"No. The Coven protects all paranormals."

"Not according to my mentor."

Sage was going to have to speak to the seer about that. He needed to expand his vampire lore because something wasn't fitting together right, and Kirk could only tell him what he knew—which was more than what Sage knew but still not enough.

"When we reach the crest, if you look left that's the ranch."

The trail widened out and then the ranch rolled out beneath them. From here it was an easy ride home. He loved this view, the endless sky and the fields. This was home, as deep in his bones as any true Madison. Maybe more so because he lived and breathed the dirt. The ranch was under his nails and in his skin.

Kirk tried to steer Donut around, but the horse was more interested in eating the shrubs than obeying its rider. Sage reached out and grabbed the rein, turning the horse around so Kirk could appreciate the view.

"It's beautiful."

Even from here they could see people moving around the ranch. No cougars, not until night. He had no doubt Kirk could see them, too. "What's your next step?"

"I'm too far away to feel their energy. I need to get down there and see if I recognize anyone."

As soon as Kirk did that, everything would sour, according to the seer. "There has to be a better way."

"You take me home for lunch and get them to file past me?"

As tempting as that was, Kirk couldn't set foot on the ranch. Sage shook his head. "We'll work something out."

"How long are they here for?"

"Another week."

Kirk blew out a breath. "I can't stay here for another week."

Can't or didn't want to?

Sage pressed his lips together and concentrated on the view. He'd known Kirk would go home and forget about him. He was just a dumb ass for hoping there would be more.

"You'll always be welcome to visit." Kirk smiled, and it was easy to believe that he meant it. But for how long would they last doing the long-distance thing? A few months? "But you can do better than a man who can't touch you the way you want. Who can't kiss you without taking a bite of your life."

But it was his damn life to risk, and so what if he wanted Kirk to take a little every time they touched. He bit his tongue and stayed quiet. They weren't logical thoughts; they were dangerous and fed on a lust that shouldn't exist.

"Give me a day to have a think, okay? We're having a hunt tonight and you don't want to be around twenty cougars all a bit twitchy because of over-crowding."

"Over-crowding?"

"As much as we like all getting together, it's actually much nicer to prowl with just one or two others. Still, tradition and all that." Some things couldn't be avoided.

"You want to shift. I can feel the animal rising in you."

"That's not an animal." He got off the horse, his jeans too tight and lust burning through his blood like a summer wildfire. "I brought lunch and a picnic blanket if you want to find out what has risen."

CHAPTER NINE

KIRK WAS DRESSED ENTIRELY in black, from his knitted hat to his boots. He could lurk in the shadows as well as any cat. Even though Sage had warned him to stay away, tonight was the perfect time to watch the ranch. He slid his binoculars into his pocket, but he carried nothing else. He didn't need a weapon when he could take a life with a touch.

And if the cougar had his throat?

He closed his eyes and breathed out. He could kill it before he suffocated. He could feed fast if needed, which was why he'd skipped wearing gloves tonight. Despite all the fur, cougars had bare skin in their ears, nose, mouth and the pads of their paws. He flexed his fingers and his knuckles cracked; not a nervous habit that he'd picked up from his mother but something about the way energy could bind up joints.

Not for the first time, he wished he'd had the chance to talk to her about what they were and what she knew. While her death couldn't be laid at the Madison's feet, Abby's was all theirs. Today's horse ride, aside from leaving him sore and stiff, had given him a feel for the land and where the best vantage points would be. He wasn't going to enter the ranch—not yet. Just watch and see if he could spot the killer.

Would he recognize the killer after so long or would all the cats look the same? He needed to find out.

He took his bike out and drove to the bridge. Then he turned off the road and entered the trail, with the lights off. He didn't need them. He could see as well as any wild animal. No bikes were allowed up the trail, but he doubted anyone would be out this late to catch him. Dressed in black, on his matt black bike he disappeared into the dark. After he'd gotten far enough that his bike was hidden from the road he pulled over. Even if he'd had a dirt bike, he wouldn't have got any further. The noise would draw attention.

With the bike ticking as it cooled beneath him, he listened. He felt for the movement in the trees. And he waited until he blended with the world around him. He couldn't hide his scent but he could melt into the shadows visually and energetically. That alone would confuse most predators. When he was sure that he gave off a signal no bigger than a squirrel, he moved. It would take him the best part of an hour to hike up to where they'd picnicked today.

He smiled as he walked, enjoying the memory, even though his heart was heavy. He was being ridiculous, playing this game with Sage. The only reason he was indulging was because Sage kept offering himself, and Kirk was so hungry he couldn't say no. He wasn't sure he would've even if he'd still been human. Sage was fun and friendly and gorgeous and everything that Kirk wanted. He even had a big extended family. And if Kirk had still been human, Sage wouldn't have looked twice at him.

Maybe.

Maybe everything would've been a whole lot simpler between them. Now it was complicated and messy and the longer it went on the worse it would get. The more it would hurt when Sage woke up and realized they could never have more than this awkward approximation of a relationship. Vampires weren't social; he was a risk to everyone around him. He doubted that the Madison cougars would welcome him with open arms.

That's why it was better Kirk just got on with finding the killer and leaving. He'd made a plan and all he needed to do was complete it. Waiting another day wouldn't change anything. What was Sage going it do? Invite him around for dinner as his boyfriend? That would go delightfully. He imagined it ending in bloodshed and death.

He wasn't boyfriend material. And he couldn't be the kind of man Sage deserved.

Kirk fisted his hands. He didn't know what kind of man he was or who he could be only that being vampire stopped him from finding out. How had his mother managed? She'd had a life and children...and even that had ended in disaster eventually.

He reached the vantage point full of bitterness and wished he'd never returned but knew he couldn't have resisted. He was here for a reason and that reason was to put Abby's death to bed for good.

He pulled out his binoculars, laydown, and waited.

————

SAGE STRIPPED off his clothes and threw them in the pile that would make it to the laundry tomorrow. His bedroom door was closed, but he could hear the growl of cougars as his family shifted and greeted each other in their other form. If he looked out of his window, he'd see them tumbling and playing like oversized housecats. They could tolerate such close quarters for short periods. Tonight, they'd scatter into the hills to run and play.

While they called it a hunt, they weren't actually allowed to bring down any deer. And the ranch animals were off limits, too. If they started killing big animals, then the cops and rangers would have to investigate and then they might start looking too closely at the ranch activities.

Sage doubted the cops would see what was right in front of them. Shifters were too farfetched. They'd never believe Abby was murdered by one either.

He shook himself then drew up the heat that made it possible for him to shift. His bones grew hot, muscles and tendons popped, and he lurched forward to land on paws. His skin prickled as fur sprouted, then he shook himself from head to tail.

It had been too long.

With a swipe of his paw on the lever handle, he opened the door and slunk out, down the stairs and out the mudroom door. All over his yard were cougars in every shade from Clay's deep rust to Mica's silver, the most common being tawny gold.

His mother was missing; she'd offered to stay with the children too young to shift instead of joining in. Shifting could be tiring, but it was fun. It was more fun with less of them on the land.

He'd managed to avoid Clay all day, not wanting to face his brother's disapproval. They'd seen each other at a distance and had both turned away. Tonight would be no different.

The seer strolled by, her fur like moonlight.

He tried to convince himself this would be great. He'd enjoyed himself at the last gathering. But he'd been twenty and it had been his first one and he hadn't had so much on his mind.

Stone barreled into him and Sage swiped at his brother's

head. He pulled his lips back and snarled. Stone tilted his head in a very human gesture and Sage sighed.

What was wrong with him?

Stone headbutted him, the silent invitation to unwind and play.

Sage returned the gesture and hoped it was convincing. He didn't want to be prowling; he wanted to be in town, in Kirk's room. In his bed. He'd thought once would be enough to get the vampire out of his system. When that hadn't worked, twice should've. They couldn't touch, but Kirk consumed all of his thoughts.

With everyone who was hunting assembled, the seer led them out. Some were obviously trying to impress her, wanting to be the next one selected as familiar. Sage wasn't sure if she chose or if she just saw the future, or if she somehow manipulated it. Maybe it was a bit of each.

He didn't know much about witches. And he knew less about vampires. He hadn't managed to talk to her today, though; she'd been busy with other things, or avoiding him. He wasn't sure which and he didn't know who else to ask. Violet had set him on this mission and left him to his own devices— which clearly wasn't a good thing because he'd fallen into bed with the vampire.

He trotted along with the pack, but his gaze was drawn to the lookout where he'd spent a few hours with Kirk. The need to be with him was a pull in his gut that he couldn't explain. He'd never felt like this about anyone.

As tempting as it was to slink away from the group and head into town in cat form, he wouldn't. For one, he'd be missed. And two, that broke the rule about no shifting in town. He refocused on the group. So, which one of the cougars here tasted like frost and pebbles and didn't care about rules if they wanted something?

THE SIGHT of twenty cougars slinking across the field was enough to create a tremor of fear that traced up Kirk's spine and lodged in the base of the skull. He watched through binoculars as they ran and tumbled. His hand bounced, keeping time with his heart.

The urge to flee was almost enough to get him up and running for safety, but not quite. He'd never outrun the cats if they found him anyway. While he might be able to fight off one or two, if they attacked en masse he wouldn't be able to fight them all off. They'd eat him before he could eat them. So he might as well sit tight and hope they didn't catch scent of him and decide to investigate.

His gaze turned to the cougar he thought was Sage; he was sure it was him. The way he moved...

Truthfully Sage could be any of them. From the darker, redder ones to the golden-browns or the pale silvery ones. From a distance they were pretty. But if he closed his eyes, he was back in the car park, the sallow light at the back of the video store casting deep shadows. Abby snarling and telling someone to, "Fuck off and find a cheerleader."

A man had laughed.

Kirk had started running, his backpack jolting with every step. He skidded to a stop at the sight of the cougar in the car park. His voice froze in his throat, and he drowned in the sensation of iced water, felt the pebbles and gin in his mouth. His sister's fear was hot and prickly.

The cat swiped her, a pale paw with long claws. She fell, kicking at the beast. The cat then grabbed her throat and shook. It was only when the animal dropped her and looked up that Kirk realized he'd taken a step forward, and was almost out of the shadows.

A noise on the street made the cat glance away and Kirk had bolted.

He opened his eyes and checked on the cats.

Pale paws. Even in the shitty light, he knew it wasn't one of the darker brown or red cougars. That left the gold and silver. There were seven names on the list, five now that Stone and Clay had been crossed off. There were six cats that were pale enough. It was those six he watched. He needed to get closer to feel them...but could he do that without giving himself away?

He scanned the area between where he lay and the house. There were several other buildings, the lodges for tourists now occupied by shifters, and the barns. The cats were heading in the opposite direction.

And then what?

If he got into the house, he'd be in the middle of Madison territory.

His other option was to take more leave from work and loiter near the driveway when they were all heading home and check each car, then follow. But he didn't like that much because he wouldn't be able to choose the time and place of the fight.

Or he could just leave and forget about revenge and justice and all the things he'd promised Abby. It wouldn't bring her back. Would it set her soul to rest? Would it change anything? He'd be able to put his own guilt to bed and stop a killer. That was worthwhile.

His gaze tracked to the cougar he believed was Sage again. He wasn't ready to walk away from him, even though that would be the smart thing to do.

No, the smart thing would've been to ignore the dragging in his gut and the need to return in the first place. To make his life in the city as best he could and forget about Madison Gully and everyone in it. Sure, he'd vowed to catch his sister's killer, but he'd been a scared fifteen-year-old.

He rubbed the faint scar on his palm—not the last blood he'd spilled for magic. But there must have been enough intent for him to be drawn back.

Gut instinct was never wrong.

He got up and didn't give himself time to have any more doubts. This needed to be over before he hurt Sage.

Down the hill through the scrub, he kept his movements as quiet as he could, his energy signature still nothing more than a squirrel. He reached the base and hunkered down, checking on the location of the cats, but he could barely see them they were so far away, melting into the night and the forest. The house was about fifty yards away. If he got caught out in the open, he wouldn't stand a chance. In the house, he could lock himself in Sage's room and pretend they were lovers.

Well, by his definition, they were.

Sprint or slink?

He dithered for a minute and then another, wishing he were running to Sage's bedroom for any other reason. He wasn't running to Sage's room tonight, though; that was not the plan, no matter the temptation.

All he wanted to do was get in a position to sense the energy of the cats as they came home, then leave when they were all in bed. Sage would never even know he was here.

He stood and moved with purpose, striding over the grass like he had every right to be there. If anyone saw him, at least they wouldn't immediately think he was a thief. They might assume he was one of the many people staying on the ranch at first glance. He'd fail the second glance. He was too short, and his hair was dark.

As he approached the house, he tried to work out the best approach. Hide beneath the porch? No, it would be too easy for them to find him and drag him out. The roof? If he got caught, he was stuck up there.

Maybe it wasn't the house he wanted, but Sage's truck. Odds were, Sage left the keys in the truck either in the ignition, or on the seat, or in the cup holder. If he was caught, he'd be able to drive away. That was a plan.

He reached the house and circled around in the shadows to where the cars were parked. At the edge of his consciousness he felt Sage, the same as always but wilder like the sun burned in his heart and gave him claws. He closed his eyes feeling for others. Chili and marmalade; Stone was with Sage. And they were close.

He needed to get to the cars. Any car with keys would do.

This time he ran hunched over, pausing to check around the corner.

He had time to draw a breath, and then he was flat on his back with a cougar on his chest. Not Sage. He was sure his heart stopped, and he forgot how to speak. He lifted his hand to defend himself, to knock the cat out with a touch.

Sage shoved the other cougar off with a headbutt and a growl.

Kirk tried to push himself up, but Sage pinned him with a large paw. The low rumble emanating from Sage made Kirk's bones shiver. The cat's claws pricked through his leather jacket as though to reinforce the point.

Between growls and tail flicks the cats conversed. Ears flattened. But Sage put himself between Kirk and Stone. Sage's claws dug deeper; his claws pierced Kirk's skin, and beads of blood formed and rolled over his chest.

"I'm guessing you don't like surprises." His voice was strained even to his ears. Too light and nervous. He was about to get eaten.

Sage glared at him, his eyes the same blue but fiercer somehow. He bared his teeth. The other cat snarled and stalked closer. A hiss from Sage finally convinced Stone to back off. Kirk tracked the cat as it went around the side of the house, then he relaxed a little. Sage's paw was still a weight on his chest, his claws painfully sharp and buried in his flesh.

"You can get off me now."

Sage lowered his head, and made what Kirk guessed was a disgruntled cougar noise. He flexed, his claws digging deeper into Kirk's skin.

"That hurts." Even though he didn't want to touch Sage, he wasn't a pin cushion, and there was the fact that the little scuffle could've drawn others. He grabbed the scruff just under Sage's ears. "Be a good kitty and get off me."

Did Sage understand? He tried to throw the cat off and failed.

He was prey, alive only because Sage wanted him to be. "Look, I know you're pissed but we can't stay here all night."

Had Stone left to get friends or to keep watch?

Did he have to knock Sage out to get away? Maybe a small jolt would be all it took to get his point across. He didn't do it very often, but he knew how to gather some of his own energy and use it like a punch or a shove. Enough to startle but not injure, though like all of his touches it could kill if he made it strong enough.

He smiled at Sage. "Unless you want me to stay the night?"

He lifted his head and kissed the cougar's nose, intending to give him an energetic shove instead of stealing a bit of life.

But that isn't what happened. He wasn't sure what when wrong, only that Sage's nose was cool and dry and the energy he'd gathered for the push burst like a water balloon on a pin.

For a moment he felt not only his shock but Sage's. Below the shock Sage was furious Kirk had trespassed, and scared that he'd be found by the man who'd killed Abby. Deeper still was an attraction that Kirk had never seen or felt in anyone. Then all of that faded to white, momentarily blinding him.

Sage stumbled back, shaking his head like it was full of bees, then sat back on his haunches. Kirk pushed up to sitting, the world moving too fast like he'd drunk champagne and the bubbles were still in his mouth and stomach. What the hell had happened?

He glanced at Sage.

Where a cat had been there was now a naked man and he looked as confused as Kirk. Sage lifted his gaze. "What did you do?"

"I tried to give you a shove to get off me." But that hadn't happened. "Are you okay?" He didn't feel like he'd accidentally fed. He wasn't sure how he felt; the world wasn't quite as tangible as it should be.

"Yeah." And it was the least convincing yes, Kirk had ever heard.

Footsteps crunched over the ground. Another man who looked vaguely familiar and yet different rounded the corner. But Kirk recognized the warmth and sweet marmalade energy that was almost swamped by annoyance. He looked too much like Sage to be anything but related.

Kirk stared up at Stone. They'd been in the same year but had little to do with each other. He was glad Stone wasn't Abby's killer. If he had been, Kirk might have gone after him that night.

That didn't mean Stone would be friendly toward him. Kirk was on Madison land, and having a fling with his younger brother

Stone glared at Kirk then dropped clothes at Sage's feet. "Everything all right?"

Sage smiled. "Yeah."

This time he sounded like he'd been having fun.

Stone's gaze flicked between the two of them, unconvinced. "You shouldn't be here. Get going and we'll forget this happened."

"I only came—"

"I don't care." Stone hooked his thumb at the driveway.

"Give us a moment." Sage pulled on pants. His hand had a tremor and he was unsettled—so unsettled Kirk felt like *he* was about to bristle with fur. Fortunately, that was impossible since he couldn't imagine anything worse—aside from being able to sense Sage's agitation in the first place.

"You don't have a moment. The others are spreading out; some will be returning and wondering what is going on. You picked a bad night for tryst." Stone glanced at Sage then took a few steps away. "I'll give a whistle if anyone comes."

Sage stood and pulled the shirt on. "Don't just sit there. Leave."

"What?" Kirk scrambled up. "I need to be here."

Sage took two steps and grabbed the front of Kirk's leather jacket. "I told you not tonight."

Kirk broke the hold but didn't put any space between them. "And what am I supposed to do? Wait until you parade them past me?"

"You don't know what you've done."

"Then tell me."

Sage shook his head, his lips pressed firmly together.

"Let me stay." Kirk wanted to reach for him, touch him... instead he fisted his hand.

For a moment, the anger in Sage's eyes settled to a simmer. "I would've invited you when it was safe. You didn't trust me."

"You're a Madison." Sage was one of them. Whatever they had was temporary.

Sage stepped back like he'd been pushed. "Take my truck. I'll get it tomorrow."

"Come with me." He extended his hand.

"No. I'm a Madison. I belong here."

Stone whistled.

"Leave before they tear you apart."

Kirk hesitated.

"Leave." There was more of the cougar snarl, but beneath it was a mountain of hurt.

Kirk crossed the few yards to the truck. He got in, knowing Sage watched him. The keys were in the ignition as expected but driving away seemed like the worst thing he could do. All he wanted to do was stay; it was a bone deep feeling much like the urge to come to Madison Gully. Maybe there was something wrong with him. He turned the key and the truck roared to life. He hadn't driven a car in years, and this one smelled of Sage.

Sage turned away as though he couldn't bear the sight of him.

That one movement was a blade between the ribs. A small but fatal wound.

They were done.

———

THE GROUND WAS cold and gritty beneath Sage's feet. His nose still tingled, and something was wrong inside of him. He could feel Kirk's dismay and the aching hurt as he left the property. He was sure he wasn't imagining the welling pain that made each breath a gasp.

"What the hell, Sage? That was Kirk?" Stone grabbed his arm.

Sage pulled free. "Leave me alone."

"He's a witch."

"He's a vampire. Nothing has happened because we can't

even touch." He stalked toward the house. "Are you happy? Even when I find someone I like, there is something in the way."

Stone followed him into the house. "Why was he here?"

"To see me." And now he was defending him. Lying for him. Who was he becoming?

The kiss on his nose, the shock and new sensations...he didn't feel good, and he wanted to blame something other than the truth. It couldn't be that. It didn't happen like this. If Kirk was a witch, that changed everything. No, Stone had to be wrong about that.

"Just drop it. If you hadn't followed maybe we'd be upstairs, and no one would've needed to know."

"He knows what we are."

"And? He's as nonhuman as we are." Sage started up the stairs.

"You're playing a dangerous game."

"I'm not playing any game." He shouldn't have started anything with Kirk. Had Kirk's trespass set the seer's trouble in motion? "He's a vampire, I'm a cougar...we're both smart enough to know it's not going anywhere."

Stone stood at the foot of the stairs. "That's not what I meant. Vampires are witches."

No, they weren't. He'd know. Wouldn't he? His nose tingled and Kirk's hurt still bled through him even though they were miles apart by now.

This wasn't happening and he wasn't having this conversation with Stone. "I'm going to bed."

"Sage."

"There's nothing to discuss. Don't get your fur ruffled." He stomped up the rest of the stairs and shut his door. He leaned against it, then rubbed his nose. If Kirk was a witch...but it hadn't been a real kiss. It was meant to be a kiss that started the familiar bond.

It had been enough of a kiss. And Stone was right.

He tipped his head back against the wood and closed his eyes. He was in more trouble than he'd ever been in. Even though there could be nothing between them, the familiar bond had formed.

Kirk was his witch. His mate.

CHAPTER TEN

WHILE SAGE HAD SLEPT, it couldn't have been called restful. He'd woken too frequently, taken too long to go back to sleep, and when he had slept, he'd dreamed of Kirk in ways that made returning to sleep even more difficult.

With the grit of coffee and sugar still on his tongue he tramped out of the house, past where his truck should've been and toward the stable where he knew his mom would be. She liked to go for a morning ride, and he'd seen her get back while drinking his second cup and hoping caffeine would make everything better. It hadn't.

His choices had been Mom or Violet, and he wasn't ready to face the seer and tell her how he'd messed up. He couldn't be the next familiar. He wasn't even a Madison. Violet saw those things and all she'd seen for him was trouble. Despite the warning he'd walked right up and embraced it. If he hadn't maybe Kirk wouldn't have trespassed. Then it wouldn't have happened.

If Kirk had listened and waited...

Mom was brushing her horse after her dawn ride. She was calm and controlled while he felt like a kitten tangled in a ball of yarn. He'd made a mess he couldn't get free of. He needed help as much as it pained him to admit. Something was most definitely wrong and if it had happened—and he wasn't sure it had—it shouldn't have happened while he was a cougar. But Kirk *had* kissed his nose.

His mind made another loop and yarn knotted tighter around him. Soon he wouldn't be able to breathe. He rubbed his nose, hoping Stone was wrong. But his hope was as fragile as a butterfly wing.

Neither of them spoke. He didn't know how to start, and Mom was brewing up something—had been for the last day. So, he waited; it would be best to let her go first.

She moved around her horse to look at him. "If you were in trouble, you'd say something?"

"Why do you think I'm in trouble?"

"The seer."

"I'm trying to stop the trouble she's seen from happening." That was the truth even though he was failing. Had failed?

Mom looked concerned, she had that pinched look that only formed when one of her boys was about to screw up and land hard. Had he already hit the ground or was he still falling? He swallowed and jumped in. "Do you know much about vampires?"

Concern became a frown. "Do you mean energy witches?"

"What?" He'd hoped she would say something to disproved Stone's comment.

She shook her head. "Calling them vampires is very rude."

"He called himself that."

Kirk was a witch? Did he know that? If he did, he'd never mentioned it and he'd seemed just as startled last night. Sage regretted sending him away, but at the time that had seemed like the safest option. "Are they really witches?"

If Kirk was a witch, then the kiss on his nose—something

that should've been nothing between them—had become everything because they were destined to be witch and familiar. He could've kissed a hundred witches and had nothing happen. He was sure some of his cousins had.

Oh, shit. That meant who ever killed Abby had been trying to get a witch. But Kirk didn't think his sister was a vampire. So what had gone wrong? Why kill her?

A shifter with a witch was a powerful thing. The bond wasn't something to be messed with. Sage had known the truth in his bones the moment it had happened but had been trying to deny it all night. He sank onto a hay bale and cradled his head in his hands.

"What's wrong?" Mom was by his side in a few steps. She squatted down and put her hand on his arm. "Are you hurt?"

A wound would be an easy fix.

"I think I'm a familiar." He could barely whisper the words. What were the odds that a witch would kiss him and that would be it, mated forever? But he remembered the seer's words—that it had to be him who helped Kirk.

Violet had known all along, but she hadn't warned him that a vampire was a witch. Was becoming a familiar the trouble she'd seen, or was there more coming?

"To an energy witch? Who?" Mom stared at him, pinning him with her gaze.

"Do you remember the Gracewells?"

"A little. Oh." Her face fell.

He couldn't stop speaking the truth now that he'd started. He needed someone to know and help him. "Mom, the sister didn't kill herself. One of us killed her. And I need to find out who."

"Why would one of us kill a witch?"

"Because she wasn't. But her younger brother was." And if any other Madison found out who Kirk was and what had happened between them, there'd be hell to pay. There were more than a few who wouldn't want Sage to be a familiar, and the killer wouldn't want Kirk getting close to the family and unmasking him. Kirk's life was in danger.

Her eyes widened. "Do you know what being a familiar means?" she hissed, her voice barely more than a whisper. "Your lives are tied together. You need to keep him safe."

"No one knows about him." They didn't know he was a witch; though how many knew vampires were witches? How long until someone realized who his lover was?

"It's a small town, Sage. And if they killed one Gracewell, they won't think anything of killing another simply to stop you from having that honor."

The worry coalesced into something colder. "But it's too late. If he dies. I die."

That would clean up the loose ends and give his cousins an edge to try and regain the ranch—unless Clay or Stone returned to work it. It wouldn't matter who died first; now that they were bound together, the result would be the same. They needed to find the killer fast.

She nodded and clasped his hands. "It's an honor to be selected by the Fates but also a burden. A responsibility to the other person. But you'll be stronger and faster, and he'll have more power too. And the closer you get, the more powerful you'll both become."

"If we accept the bond...the Coven can break it." He'd heard it was possible, a safeguard in case a witch and a shifter accidentally created a bond neither wanted. They'd be safer alone. Except the Coven hunted vampires.

She stared at him. "Why wouldn't you accept it? You've been chosen."

Had he? Or had he stumbled into something without realizing? "Kirk doesn't know a vampire is a witch."

"Why wouldn't he? Did he kiss you or did you kiss him? Not that it matters." She ruffled his hair as though proud of this accident.

"He said the Coven hunts his kind. Do they?" If they did, he was stuck with the bond. What would happen to them?

She shook her head. "The Coven only hunts those who are hurting people or putting us all in danger."

Did feeding off people count as hurting them? He needed to speak to Kirk. They needed to talk about the bond and trap the killer before he trapped them. "Can you give me a ride into town? I left my truck there."

She lifted one eyebrow and gave him a look that suggested she saw through the tissue thin lie. "You should talk to Violet first."

"No. I was supposed to help Kirk, not become his mate." Violet would've warned him, wouldn't she?

Besides Kirk probably didn't want to see him again after the way he'd behaved last night. He'd had blood on his fingernails when he'd shifted to human. If he did nothing, he'd end up with blood on his hands. He wasn't just helping Kirk now; he was protecting him from the shifter who'd killed Abby.

———

KIRK WAS gritty eyed and on a knife edge. He cracked his knuckles again unable to stop. He didn't know exactly what had happened, but he knew his mentor hadn't been full of shit when he'd said that some shifters helped vampires become stronger. That there was a certain magic between them. His mentor had spent a good part of his time searching for that shifter, and he had fortunately never found them.

But Kirk had, and completely by accident.

Within him he could feel Sage's agitation, the cat lashing at the confines. He scrubbed his hand over his face. He didn't want this. He didn't want extra power that came at the expense of Sage. When Sage realized they had this bond he'd call the Coven to deal with Kirk. The Coven would ensure there was one less vampire in the world. There couldn't be many of them left.

His phone buzzed with a message from Sage.

Stay indoors. Safe. Do not engage with any Madison.

Yesterday the messages had been flirty and fun. Today they were orders. Well, the diner was technically indoors. Was it safe? Not for the humans while he was here. He'd already had a nibble off the waitress. He'd barely touched his pancakes, but the coffee was helping him think.

Except he hadn't come up with a single idea that would help. All he wanted to do was be with Sage. Sage was going to be pissed.

The message flashed up again and Kirk replied. *At the diner.*

The waitress poured a second cup and Kirk smiled and thanked her. He forced down another bite of syrup drenched pancake. His stomach turned as though he were already too full. Was this it? No more food? He wasn't ready to lose that small pleasure. He'd thought he had a few more years.

The moment he'd put his lips on Sage's nose, everything had gone wrong, and he hadn't even gotten the chance to feel out the rest of the shifters. The whole mission had been a terrible failure and he didn't know how to salvage any part of it. Maybe he couldn't.

The door chimed as it swung open, just like the first time Sage strolled in and sat at his table. This time, there was a tension around his eyes and in the set of his jaw, but he looked more tired than furious.

His gaze landed on the pancakes. "You eating that?"

Kirk pushed the plate over, unable to take another bite.

"Why did you order if you weren't going to eat?"

"I thought I could." He needed to say something. "Last night..."

Sage looked up and put the fork down. He leaned over the table. "Not here. As it is, they're making up tales about our relationship."

They didn't have one. They'd known each other for a few days. Yet with Sage opposite him the jangling in Kirk's bones faded to a hungry need to reach out and touch him. He stretched out his legs, so his jean covered calf brushed Sage's. Sage smiled.

"I think I can manage another bite." The hunger for food was back. If he was only hungry around Sage, that was really going to suck when he returned home. The need to be near Sage would make riding away hurt.

Sage broke off a forkful and offered it to him.

Kirk leaned forward and accepted the mouthful, enjoying the sweetness. It wouldn't last. He looked up at Sage. "You should hate me."

Sage drew in a breath as though drawing up strength. "Do you not listen to anything I say? Even when it's for your own good?"

"I don't know what happened," Kirk whispered. "Whatever it was it was an accident."

Sage considered him for several seconds, then he nodded as though he'd determined that Kirk was telling the truth. "Let's finish off."

He finished the pancake in a few bites, then pulled out his wallet and left enough to cover the breakfast and tip the waitress generously.

Kirk downed the rest of his coffee in a few swallows and got up to follow Sage outside. The world was sharper today.

Brighter. As though he'd been seeing it through gray tinted glasses.

If he reached out, he'd be able to hold Sage's hand...and kill him. If not in seconds, then definitely in minutes.

"Your truck's at the B&B."

"I know; I went past there first. Then I got Mom to drop me here."

They walked up the sidewalk, not talking about the thing that breathed between them. It burned Kirk's tongue until he had to speak. "I didn't mean for it to happen."

If he kept apologizing, would that make it right, or would Sage still turn him over to the Coven?

"What do you think happened?"

"Some shifters can be bound and used for extra power. My mentor tried several times. He didn't want to die and had been hoping a shifter would buy him more time." The killing had become too much. No one's life was worth so much death.

Sage winced. "And you?"

Kirk shook his head. "I stopped him."

He hoped the way he said it was weighted enough for Sage to understand that when he said stop, he meant killed.

They continued in silence again, but it was comfortable. Friendly almost. Not what he'd been expecting. "You aren't going to call the Coven?"

Sage stopped. "Why would I?"

"So they can hunt me down..." He was missing something. "You aren't angry with me. You know what's going on."

"You haven't bound me. I'm not trapped in my other form, am I?"

No, Sage was very much a man this morning. "But there's something. I can feel it."

"It's called the familiar bond and it works both ways. It

makes witch and shifter both stronger. In my family, it's an honor to be a witch's familiar. But not all shifters believe that."

"I'm not a witch."

"Who told you that?"

They turned the corner and Sage's truck came into view. His mentor had called him a vampire. The word witch had only ever been used when talking about the Coven. His mother had never used those words. What they were had never been discussed.

His mentor had warned him against socializing with other paranormals in case they worked out what he was. But the lie that had kept him chained was now broken. Maybe it wasn't to protect him; it was so he didn't learn the truth. He stared at his hands and the scars on his knuckles.

How much of what he'd learned and believed was lies?

"I'm not a vampire?"

"You are...but I was told that it's rude to call you that. Energy witch is more correct."

"And what does that mean?"

"I don't know. I do know witches have different talents. That they deal with animals or plants or healing. And some can read minds and others can grant wishes for a price."

"I know about nature witches. My mentor would sneer at them feeding on plants and animals and obeying the Coven. Maybe I was supposed to be like that, and he broke me." Kirk's stomach turned, and the pancakes sunk in a sea of turbulent black coffee.

"Violet, our seer, would know more. I'm going to have to talk to her anyway. This is an accidental bond...she always sees who's going to be the next familiar. It shouldn't have been me. I'm not even a Madison. This is a mess."

Kirk shook his head; Sage was wrong about the seer. "She made sure we'd meet. That you'd help me."

Sage frowned. "What are you saying?"

"That she set us up. I was drawn back here the same weekend you're having your family gathering. I thought it was old ghosts and revenge that drew me back. But...I think it was you."

"You think Violet saw me as the next familiar? Why would I get that honor?"

"Why couldn't it be you? It's not just Madison shifters that can become familiars, right? So Violet saw the next connection and helped it happen. Maybe that's what she does. She picks the shifter most likely to find their mate."

"But it's supposed to be announced before it happens."

"I didn't know it would happen. I just wanted to get you off of me. You put holes in me."

"I was angry at you and worried that you'd be caught. I'm sorry."

"It's okay, I heal fast. My jacket doesn't."

Sage glanced at his truck. "Where's your bike?"

"Up the trail a bit." He hadn't been back to fetch it, figuring it was safe for the moment. "I was being careful. I was going to get in your truck and watch and wait then slink away when you'd all gone to bed. I need to know who killed Abby." He still wanted the killer brought to justice. He wanted Sage to know that the murder hadn't been forgotten and it would never be forgiven. "He knew that my family was vampires...witches, even though we didn't know." If his mother had known, she'd never breathed a word. Maybe she'd been like his mentor, expecting to be hunted down. "He thought Abby was a witch."

"Which means he'll know you are."

It wasn't the Coven coming after him that Kirk had to worry about. It was the killer wanting a witch.

"But I already have a familiar."

"They won't be too happy with that, if they want a witch."

Sage licked his lip. "Our lives our bound now. If one of us dies—"

"We both die." He knew that bit. His mentor had said that finding the one meant taking care of it. He'd done something to the shifters he'd caught to keep them animals, locked them up and fed on them until they'd died hoping to find the one. If Kirk had known sooner, if he hadn't been so scared...he should've contacted the Coven, but he didn't know how. He was glad his mentor had never been successful. But had no idea how or why he'd gotten a familiar. "Why was I chosen?"

Sage shrugged. "Violet might know. Maybe there's no reason. The Fates tossed their dice and here we are."

"Then what do we do next? Would it be safer to leave?" But he'd come here to find a killer and running didn't seem like the right thing to do.

"Violet said trouble is coming, and that I need to help you. I think we have to stick to the plan."

There was only one problem with that. "We don't have a plan."

"Sure we do. We go get your bike, we meet with Violet, and then I find a way to parade the suspects by you." Sage opened his truck door and glanced at the ignition. "Where's the keys?"

Kirk pulled them out of his pocket and tossed them over. He wanted to be able to put them in Sage's hand. Could he touch him now that they shared a bond? "And what about us?"

"What do you mean?"

Kirk got into the truck and shut the door. "I mean is this just a magic thing or more?"

Sage smiled. "It's what we want to make of it. It can be a working relationship only, but for the Madisons it's usually more."

Usually. But as Sage had said he wasn't really a Madison.

For all of Sage's calm exterior, beneath was turmoil. Roiling emotions he didn't know what to do with. Kirk could sense his tail lashing and the snarl forming. Was he annoyed that his mate was a vampire, or stressed about the killer? No matter the cause it set Kirk's teeth on edge. He reached out and put a hand on Sage's leg.

Sage glanced at him. "What are you doing?"

"I don't know." He pulled his hand back. "You're agitated and growling." And he'd wanted to sooth that somehow and promise it would all work out. But like his vow to Abby he didn't know if he'd be able to keep it.

"I wasn't." Sage started the truck. "Okay I was. How did you know that?"

"I can feel it." Which was disconcerting at best.

"Touch me again."

No matter how much he longed to hear those words he still hesitated. "Are you sure?"

"Yes."

Kirk cautiously put his hand on Sage's thigh, the thin layer of denim all that protected him. The cougar calmed. "Is your inner cougar always at odds with you?"

"It's not my inner cougar. It's me, just the other me." He pulled on to the street and headed toward the bridge. "I don't know what's going on. I don't know what Violet will say. My mom is stressed out and my brothers are pissed with me. You know Stone. And Clay was spying on you the other day."

"They seem delightful." At least Sage had family to be annoyed at and who cared about him.

"I will always be their much younger baby brother. They'll be eighty and still treating me like I'm five."

"Do they always check out your boyfriends?"

"Clay's a cop, so probably. If I tell them. Most of the time it's not worth it." Sage parked the truck off the road near the bridge. "How far up the trail?"

"Not that far. You don't have to come."

"I'm not letting you out of my sight. What if the killer jumps you? You didn't fight Stone or me off effectively last night."

"I knew it was you. I didn't want to hurt you." Even when Sage's claws had pressed into his skin.

"Why did you kiss my nose?"

"To give you a shock, that was all. It wasn't even really a kiss. I just wanted skin on skin for it to work." And it had seemed like the right thing to do at the time.

"Well, something worked."

But would they? This was all new to Kirk. He was a witch, not just a vampire. And now he had a familiar. A mate. And all that entailed. His life no longer sounded so hollow.

They got out of the car and walked up the trail. He was able to enjoy it more on foot than he had on horseback or while creeping last night. The leaves crunched beneath his feet, and the air was sharp and cold and clear, different to the dirty taste the car fumes left in his mouth.

With Sage striding next to him, everything that had bothered him fell away. For those moments they were the only people in existence, and nothing mattered but what they wanted. He glanced at Sage and smiled. Sage returned the smile, having been caught looking. Pink spread over Sage's cheeks and he looked away first.

Maybe because this was fated, it would all work out. Kirk tried to imagine a life with someone. He hadn't ever let himself hold those thoughts; now that he could he didn't know what to do with them. Did he let his imagination go wild or did he hold back?

He exhaled; he'd talk to the Madison seer and get some more information and then they could make a plan. And if the killer found them in the meantime...

"Do you really think one of your relatives would attack me?"

Sage glanced up at the sky peeking through the leaves. "They might if they find out about the bond."

"But that would hurt you." And Sage clearly thought Abby had been killed because of magic she didn't possess.

"There are some who wouldn't care if I dropped dead. There are divisions in the family; some stuff went down when I was a kid and I think people are still angry."

"And Abby got mixed up because they thought having a witch would help?"

"Possibly. Without asking the killer we won't know for sure."

"Hang on. You said the Coven could undo this."

"It's not painless, but there is a way. In the past witches used to find their familiar and keep them because it made them powerful."

Kirk lifted his eyebrows and feigned surprise. "The shifters didn't want it?"

"Not always. Do you not want this?"

"I don't know. I don't know anything." His whole world had been shaken and he was still trying to determine what it looked like. His mind was racing with what-ifs from twenty years ago. What if he'd been caught by the cougar who'd killed his sister. Would he have been locked in a basement the way his mentor had done? "Do shifters keep witches in much the same manner?"

"There was a spate of witch trappings, decades ago. Payback for centuries of mistreatment. But the Coven didn't allow that either."

They rounded a bend and tucked to the side was Kirk's bike. Relief washed through him that it was still there with all its parts attached.

"I don't know anything about bikes, but it looks nice." Sage grinned.

Kirk walked over and knelt by the bike. "It looks like I won't be offering you a ride back down. Both tires have been slashed."

Sage joined him. But he studied the ground, not the bike, seeing things Kirk couldn't comprehend. "One man did this."

"One shifter." It was a pity he couldn't feel any residual energy. For that he'd need to be psychic. Maybe there was a kind of witch that could touch things and see the past.

"Yeah." Sage glanced around. "Your visit last night was noticed by more than Stone and me."

Kirk reached out feeling for any creature that didn't belong. For the energy of a Madison. for anything that didn't belong. "And if they found my bike then they'll know it's me. I doubt there's another like this in town."

"This is quad bike and truck territory." Sage stood. "I'll help you get it back down the hill."

That solved the problem in the short term, but not how he was going to get home. "I can't leave town until I replace the tires." That wasn't going to be cheap.

"I can drive you into the city...but this needs sorted first." He offered Kirk a hand.

Kirk didn't reach out and take it, even though he wanted to. Sage stood there hand out, as though refusal wasn't an option but he should know better.

Kirk shook his head. "I'm not safe to touch."

"Humor me."

"Why?" All the little touches would add up. He'd tire Sage out until Sage actually started dying, just like Kirk's father. The doctors hadn't been able to treat him because they hadn't known what was causing his illness—and wouldn't have believed it even if they'd been told. His mother's love killed his father.

But not Abby or him.

"Because it might be different now." Sage kept his hand out.

"And it might not be. I'm broken."

"You're not."

Kirk wanted nothing more than to grab Sage's hand and be pulled into his embrace. He wanted to believe that Sage was right, and that they could touch because of the bond. The ache to be able to touch and have a lover consumed him. "I don't want to hurt you."

"Our lives are linked. You won't." But hesitation vibrated around Sage.

"You don't know for sure."

"Neither do you. But it would be nice to know, wouldn't it?" Sage smiled, his eyes bright as though he knew he'd won the argument.

Kirk reached out and clasped Sage's hand.

CHAPTER ELEVEN

SAGE HOPED he wasn't wrong. That what he'd heard about the familiar bond wasn't all gossip and superstition—both of which could hold a measure of truth but were often filled out with nothing more than wishful thinking. This honor shouldn't have been his, but he didn't want to let it go. He liked the idea that they were meant to be together.

Kirk stared up at him, his whisky eyes filled with confusion. Sage could feel Kirk's uncertainty mirroring his own. This was all new to both of them. Between them they didn't have enough information, but he was willing to test some theories.

Kirk clasped his hand. There was the now familiar jolt of static as their skin connected, the spark traced down his spine as though a hand ruffled his fur. He pulled Kirk up and to him, trusting Kirk not to take more than a trickle of his energy, his life.

"Our lives are bound." He kept hold of Kirk's hand, tempting trouble.

"I can feel that." He held Sage's gaze.

Sage couldn't feel Kirk in that way, but he sensed the witch's curiosity and his caution as though it were his own. If he could feel Kirk emotions, maybe Kirk could feel his. He focused on the other things he was feeling.

They were alone. They could steal a few moments for themselves before facing the rest of the world. He wanted to know what it was like to kiss Kirk. He wanted more than just a business relationship with his witch. He didn't know if that was possible, though, given Kirk's deadly ability. But they were still holding hands and he didn't feel faint or weak, so he was ready to push the boundaries further.

Kirk's eyes widened as though he'd read Sage's thoughts not just his emotions. His tongue darted over his lower lip. His fingers flexed as though he wanted to pull away, but Sage held on.

He wasn't dizzy or drained. "Tell me you don't want this, that you don't want to be lovers, and I won't ask again."

Kirk closed his eyes. "I wish I could. If I was a better person, I'd push you away, find a way to break thi—"

Sage closed the distance and ducked his head to kiss him. Their lips connected with a spark that sent a tingle to his toes. *Still not dead or dying.*

He waited for Kirk to respond. One heartbeat, two. Nothing. The pain ricocheted through him and settled in his gut. He eased back, trying to mask the hurt. He'd thought this was something Kirk wanted.

"I don't know what I'm doing," Kirk mumbled, staring at the ground. "It's been over a decade since I've let anyone close enough to kiss me."

"How much are you holding back so you don't drain me?" Was this really dangerous and stupid?

"It feels different this time. Like I don't have hold back because I'm plugged into a loop. It's flowing between us." His eyebrows knitted together. "It's weird."

"Magical?"

The corners of his lips tilted up. "Maybe. Can we try the kiss again?"

Sage didn't bother with words. His lips connected with Kirk's and this time Kirk's mouth moved, cautiously as though he had to remember how to kiss. Sage nudged him along with little tastes, before dipping his tongue into Kirk's open mouth. Lust spiraled through him and Kirk's desire fanned the flames.

Kirk's hand slid around Sage's neck as he pressed closer, their linked hands now in the way between them. He pulled free and gripped Kirk's hip so he could press against him. Kirk tasted like coffee and smelled like sex. He wanted more of him, all of him.

This was his mate, and no one—not even the seer—could tell him it wasn't right. His throat vibrated like he wanted to purr, and he curled his fingers into the denim covering Kirk's ass. Kirk moaned against his lips and ground against his hips.

"You want more?" Sage wanted everything.

"Yeah. But—"

"I'm fine. You're fine. And we can stop anytime."

Kirk nodded. "What do you want? I don't have anything with me."

"Don't need condoms for what I have in mind." Sage drew back just enough to undo Kirk's belt. Kirk hadn't let anyone close for a very long time, and while Sage could think of a few things he wanted to do, he thought it would be best to start slowly, safely.

He flicked open the top button then dragged down the zipper. "I want to suck you."

Kirk inhaled sharply. "Are you sure? What if it does something else?"

Sage slid his hand into Kirk's briefs and let his fingertips stroke the hard length of his dick. "Did the kiss change anything?"

He hadn't felt a change, but he wasn't sensitive to energy shifts like Kirk.

Kirk shook his head. "Not that I could tell. I don't think I can feed on you...because it would be like feeding on myself if that makes sense?"

It made as much sense as accidentally finding his mate and Sage was willing to hold onto that fluke. Not because it would give him extra abilities but because he was able to glimpse a life where he didn't end up alone on the ranch.

And if the seer insisted this be broken because it wasn't what she'd seen? He'd refuse. The bond wasn't the kind of thing that should be thrown away if both witch and shifter wanted the connection. They'd find a way to make this work because it was meant to be. And if nothing else, Sage believed in magic and fate and love.

Sage freed Kirk's dick from the fabric and caressed the length. He liked the way the shaft curved up and that pre-come already slicked the head. He rubbed his thumb over the slit, imagining the taste in his mouth.

"You want to lean on your bike?"

Kirk took a step back and rested his hands behind him on the seat of the bike.

Sage stole another kiss, Kirk's movements more confident with every passing heartbeat, then he kissed down his witch's neck before dropping to his knees in front of him. He glanced up taking in the sight, the ruddy, hard dick begging for attention and the way Kirk watched him with dark eyes. Sage wasn't sure if he'd ever wanted to do this as much as he did in that moment.

He never wanted to forget this. The molten heat in Kirk's gaze, the nip in the air, and the way the trees rustled softly as though breathing with them. Sage licked along the length, tasting the salty spill that trickled along the underside before taking him in his mouth.

"Ah, fuck," Kirk whispered like a prayer.

Sage smiled as best he could with his mouth full, determined to give Kirk something to really swear about. He took him deeper, sucking as he drew back, pressing the tip to the roof of his mouth and then using his tongue to worship the head. Kirk leaked a little more pre-come into Sage's mouth. He didn't usually swallow, but this time he didn't want to pull away.

The scent of Kirk's arousal filled his lungs and pulsed within him. His own dick was like rock, but for the moment that didn't matter. He'd had plenty of sex over the years, and Kirk had gone without, afraid that he'd hurt his lover.

There was only a nibble of doubt that something could go wrong, but it was enough for Sage to pay attention to every move Kirk made. Including the way he started to rock his hips and the way his breath caught. The lust that wrapped around them was a living thing, quickening Sage's heartbeat and making him hungry for more. He wanted Kirk to come.

He glanced up and became lost in Kirk's eyes. Had a lover ever looked at him so intently? Sage drew back so he could lick around the head and press his tongue to the slit as though demanding more.

"I can't hold back." Kirk's words were breathy nothings.

Sage took him deep, looking up at him. He knew the moment before it happened, but he couldn't have said how. Kirk gasped, and his hips bucked as he came. Sage's mouth filled and he swallowed, continuing to work Kirk over until he was done. Then he licked him clean before pulling away. Kirk's chin rested on his chest as he gasped for air. Sage waited a moment before gently tucking Kirk's dick back into his briefs.

Kirk stopped him before he could do up his jeans, his hand over Sage's. "Thank you."

"It was just as fun for me." And he meant it. He'd felt Kirk's lust and heady tumble over the edge as though it were his own. But it was the way Kirk had watched him that would remain.

This wasn't a quick hook up to take away the edge. And there was more between them that just magic.

Kirk lifted his head and looked at Sage as though the whole concept of sex being fun was alien. Maybe it was with every interaction tainted by risk. His eyebrows drew together, and he pulled Sage up. "You're still okay?"

"Better than." He almost felt as good as if he'd come. He hadn't, he was still hard and aching, but that could wait. One step at a time. What would it feel like if he had lost too much of his life? He didn't feel ill or tired. He drew in a breath. He'd never felt more alive.

"Shall we?" Sage tilted his head at the path back down the mountain.

"You don't want anything in return?"

He closed his eyes for a heartbeat. "I do, but it can wait. That was for you." He gave Kirk a grin. "I really wanted to see you lose a little of that steely control."

———

BETWEEN THE TWO OF THEM, they got the bike in the bed of the truck. A blanket from the cabin protected the paintwork, but Kirk still didn't like seeing his bike wrapped up like it was injured. Tomorrow morning he'd call the repair shop and get two tires put aside, then convince Sage to drive him to the city.

He glanced at Sage as he drove, knowing he'd already messaged the seer telling her that they needed to talk. Talking was the last thing Kirk wanted to do. He wanted to be with Sage, just the two of them, figuring this thing out.

Kirk couldn't remember ever letting go so completely and he hadn't hurt Sage at all. He cracked his knuckles, sure he could still feed off others, but while he could feel Sage's energy rubbing against his own like an overly friendly cat, he couldn't do much more than play with it. Even if he'd wanted to use it, he didn't know how.

"What are you doing?"

Kirk looked over. "Nothing, why?"

"You were doing something. It felt like you were touching me."

"You were rubbing up against me. I was reciprocating."

Sage took his eyes off the road, his eyebrows pinched together. "My hands have stayed on the steering wheel. What do you mean?"

"Your body is, but your energy, the stuff I feel and feed off, is leaning into me, purring."

"You feel it as my cat?"

He hadn't last night when Sage had been a cat. "When you're human."

"Huh. And you knew it was me last night because you felt the man?"

"No. I felt your energy signature and knew it was you; it's the same no matter your body. The same way I knew it was Stone even though I hadn't seen him for years. Everyone is unique. I guess it's like the way you can smell people. You'd never get two mixed up."

Sage didn't turn towards the B&B as expected, instead he turned toward the cemetery.

"Where are we going?"

"Somewhere we can talk to Violet without the risk of being overheard."

"You managed to sneak up on me when I was at the cemetery."

"If I'd done a good job of it, you wouldn't have known I was there."

"I can sense people long before they get close." When he'd been at school that had saved him from the school bullies more than once. He'd thought he was just hyper vigilant. Now he knew it had been the start of his magic manifesting. The bullies had eventually turned their attention elsewhere because he wasn't an easy target.

"So we'll be fine. The killer won't look for us there. He'll know where you're staying—the town isn't that big. I think your bike was a warning."

"A warning that means I can't leave, now I'm trapped and nowhere in town is safe." He should borrow Sage's truck and go, even though it was the last thing he wanted to do.

"Nowhere. Period."

"You think I'll be hunted?"

Sage glanced over. "I think it's a possibility if he wants a witch. And I think we're stronger together."

"But you don't know that."

"Which is why we'll talk to the seer and figure out this bond."

"If they come after me, and kill me—"

"Then I'll die," Sage said. "Best make sure you don't get killed."

"So, we should break the bond. It would be safer." But he didn't want to do that either. What if this was Kirk's only chance to have something close to normal? That wasn't the right reason to keep Sage glued to his side, though. "We barely know each other."

Sage pulled into the cemetery car park. "If you'd been all

excited to have a familiar, I'd have been a whole lot more troubled. That you're questioning this is reassuring."

He put his hand on Kirk's thigh and Kirk's first thought was to brush him off. He wasn't used to the casual touches. He drew in a breath and let Sage's hand rest on his thigh, the heat of his palm soaking through.

"Let's just see what Violet has to say." Sage's smiled faded to something grimmer.

"You're worried about something."

Sage bit his lower lip and stared out the windscreen. "Yeah. What if she wants this bond broken?"

"Why would she?" *Oh.* "Because I'm a vampire."

"You're a witch."

"Just the wrong kind." What kind should he have been? Who could he have been if his mentor hadn't taken him in? How many people would he have accidentally hurt if left on his own, untrained like his mother?

Sage didn't answer. He got out of the truck, leaving Kirk with his darkening thoughts. What if he couldn't be fixed and he was what he was, the kind of witch that the Coven hunted and put down because he was dangerous, just like his mentor said. Maybe there was some truth in those lies.

He watched Sage pace and could feel the agitation prickling against his skin even though Sage looked calm, thumbs hooked in his pockets as he waited. Eyes as blue as the sky. He was too...wholesome was the only word Kirk could come up with. People like Sage Madison didn't end with people like him whose family tree was short, stunted, and mostly dead. Kirk may not be the poor kid of the school cleaner anymore, but he wasn't *mate* material.

He still wasn't sure what this all entailed only that it didn't seem like a good idea to tie one's life to another. His mentor had killed seeking this bond. They were assuming Abby's killer had also wanted this. Had the killer hoped to force the bond much like his mentor?

Kirk got out and leaned on the hood, but his gaze swung to where Abby rested.

This was all about her. She'd have hated that. She'd have punched him in the arm and told him to get a life. It had been a long time since he'd missed her so keenly.

A small golden hatchback pulled up. Kirk straightened and flexed his fingers.

Sage put his hand on Kirk's forearm. There were too many layers of clothing between them, but at the same time not enough to keep his heart safe. He shouldn't be falling for Sage, but he didn't know how to stop. They were bound together, and Sage didn't fear him. He wanted him. That was more than enough for Kirk. More than he'd ever let himself dream of.

"It's okay; it's Violet," Sage said with a smile that was betrayed by the tension that wound between them.

Kirk relaxed a little but remained on guard. He didn't know the seer and wasn't sure she could be trusted. He reached out as far as he could searching for anyone, or any cougar, that could be close enough to overhear. But they were alone with only the dead to eavesdrop.

The seer got out of the car. An older woman with long white hair, she moved with grace and a bounce that he recognized from Sage. Her gaze flicked between them both and her expression went from intrigued to concerned.

"Oh...this is rather more complicated than I thought it would be."

CHAPTER TWELVE

THERE WAS no point in denying the bond to the seer, so Sage leaped in to defend himself and Kirk. "I know you hadn't announced who the next familiar would be, and I didn't expect it to happen, but Kirk is my witch."

Violet nodded. "I can see that."

"It was an accident," Kirk added.

"These things are never accidents." She turned her attention to Sage. "But you're supposed to wait until it's announced."

"You didn't say that. You didn't warn me. Just sent me off to help him find out who killed his sister—which we still don't know. And now his tires have been slashed and he's stuck in town." The words tumbled out, pushed by the fear that everything was coming undone and he'd end up with nothing.

"Wait. You knew about this? That Sage is my familiar?" Kirk asked.

Sage stared at Kirk as it clicked for him. She had said something about waiting.

Violet shook her head. "I saw a connection was about to be made. I knew it would be you, Sage, and I was happy for you, so

I encouraged it. But I also knew that your mate would bring trouble, only I didn't know what. It's starting to make sense."

He was supposed to be the chosen familiar? How could it be him when he shared a name, not blood, with the Madison family?

"Whoever killed Abby thought she was a vampire...er, witch," Kirk corrected himself. "Until we know who that is, Sage is in danger because of me."

"I agree. I don't think it would be wise to say anything to anyone until we know who attacked you sister," Violet said.

"You haven't seen who the killer is?" Sage pressed. What good was a seer if she missed the important things?

"I can't see the past. I knew the Gracewells were witches, and I knew that their fate would be tied with ours somehow. Abby's death was covered up, and I'm sorry that I didn't challenge the lies. But I don't know if I could've done anything differently, or if anyone would've believed me." She turned to Kirk. "There were no witnesses...or at least none that came forward at the time. I don't blame you for that."

"I thought my promise to Abby had drawn me back. But I'm not sure now."

"It doesn't matter why you came back, only that you did. Timing is everything and twenty years ago you were both kids. Running was probably the best thing you could've done." She took a step closer. "Show me your hands."

Kirk held them out, knuckles up so she could see the scars. "Can the bond be broken, to protect Sage?"

Even if it could be broken, Sage didn't want that. He wanted Kirk.

She smiled. "That's sweet of you to ask, but only if you haven't slept together. So...I'm guessing no."

Sage stared at the ground and tried to will the heat from his cheeks.

"The urge to complete the bond is strong." She didn't touch Kirk's hands, but she studied the scars.

"Can it be forced?" Had someone hoped to trap Abby? Who in his family would want an unwilling witch?

Violet glanced at Sage. "If you'd paid more attention to our history..." She sighed. "Yes. For centuries witches kept shifters as pets, and some were able to force a bond. Not all witches are good. But we also understood how valuable the familiar bond can be when done willingly. For the witch and for us. The bond was protection from those who'd do us ill." She looked Kirk in the eye and said, "Whoever did this to you twisted your magic."

"An evil witch wouldn't come near the family if there was a good witch there," Sage said, remembering a little of the history lessons. That made sense. "That doesn't explain how you can predict it."

"That was gift bestowed by a witch a long time ago. It passes through my line. An almost magic that is never guaranteed, but always right. Announcing the next familiar makes it that much more special, and then I tell the familiar what I know about their witch to make it easier for them to find, though in truth what I see is merely converging lines of fate. I saw the threads of this years ago but didn't know what to make of it."

"That's all very lovely, but what do you do when you get stuck with an evil witch?" Kirk cracked his knuckles as if to prove the point.

Sage put his hand over Kirk's. That snap was there, but it didn't hurt. It didn't bother him at all. Kirk couldn't feed on him; Kirk wasn't evil or broken or any of the other things he used to describe himself. He had a few magical issues, but that didn't matter to Sage.

Violet considered Kirk for what felt like a lifetime. "You aren't evil. You were trained wrong. Taught to be a vampire."

"My mentor was a vampire. He said other witches hunted those like us."

"That is true; the Coven does hunt down those witches, those shifters, those anything, that hurt others. Those who kill and take delight in pain are caught and punished. The Coven are our police. The man who did this to you was probably wanted by them. But how many have you willingly killed?"

Sage held his breath, wishing he'd asked that question earlier so he wouldn't be shocked when Kirk answered.

"None. I feed in crowds, a little from everywhere."

"See? Not evil." Violet smiled as though everything were solved.

Sage ran his thumb over the scars on Kirk's knuckles. "Will he always be a vampire?"

"I don't know. Only the Coven would be able to answer that."

Kirk shook his head and stepped back, breaking the contact. Fear rippled off him. "They'll kill me."

"No, they won't. Trust me. Trust us," Violet urged him.

Sage looked at Kirk and understood his caution. There was no reason for him to the trust the Madison cougars. "We'll catch Abby's killer and sort this out. One thing at a time."

"How? I need to be close enough to feel his energy. I wouldn't know him on sight. And how many will take my word for it?"

"I will," Sage said. Kirk's worry thrummed through him like an off-kilter purr that set his teeth on edge.

"As will I," Violet chimed in. "For the moment, no one is to learn you are mates."

That horse might have bolted. "I said something to Mom."

"And she spoke to me. She won't say anything."

"His brother pounced on me last night," Kirk added.

Violet flicked her hand dismissively. "Pfft. Booty call."

"Stone knew Kirk was a witch." And Sage was reasonably sure Stone wasn't thrilled his baby brother was having fun with one.

"Of course, he did. There's just something..." Her eyes narrowed. "All paranormals have an..."

"Energy?" Kirk offered.

She shrugged. "Near enough. Feeling your own kind is easy; witches usually aren't too hard either. You're different. You don't smell like a witch either. That might protect you a bit."

But not for long. His name would be familiar to the killer... but only Mom, Stone and Violet knew Kirk's name. "How tight is the bond?"

"Don't get killed would be my recommendation."

"You can't see a solution? Or find the killer?" Sage pressed.

"No. I see possible familiar bonds." She shook her head. "I'm sorry I can't be more help."

But Sage knew that wasn't all; she was hiding something. After the trouble her half-truths had created, it irked him like a thorn between the toes of his paws that he couldn't pull out.

Kirk crossed his arms, hiding his hands. "I need access to the ranch, to check everyone."

"I'll have to talk to some of the other senior cougars, but I'm sure something can be arranged. I want this settled before I announce this gathering's familiar."

There would be some who wouldn't be happy that he was getting the honor when he barely shared the name. Sage glanced at the seer again. She saw potential connections. "You give people a nudge when you see a potential connection?"

"Yes, to make sure it happens."

"Which is why you said it had to be me who helped Kirk."

"Yes," she answered more cautiously.

Kirk was staring at him, too.

Sage wasn't quite sure if he was on the right path or about to drive off the edge of a cliff. "So, what happens when you don't think the shifter would make a good familiar?"

Violet considered him for a moment before responding, "Then I find ways to discourage the connection."

"You could've warned me that Kirk was my mate."

"No, then it becomes a forced thing. It needs to happen naturally." She glanced at Kirk. "Did you feel the pull?"

Kirk nodded. "Did you draw me here?"

"No, but not everyone ends up where they're supposed to be."

Sage pursed his lips and tried to find a way to get the conversation back on track. "Who had a possible connection, but you discouraged it?"

"Mica. But he never knew. I don't say anything until I'm sure. I wasn't sure about this, not because of you Sage, but..."

"Because of me." Kirk finished for her and she had the decency to look abashed.

"You can't feel the trouble brewing?" Violet asked them. "There will be blood spilled before this is done."

"How many possible familiars are there each gathering?"

"Sometimes none, sometimes only one, sometimes more than one. But it also depends on how close the connection is. I'm not going to send someone on a quest halfway around the world because their witch lives in Australia. The odds of that bond working out are so small it's not worth the chance." She lifted her hands and shrugged. "It's a delicate art."

"You're playing with people's lives," Kirk said. His face was neutral but beneath the cool exterior he was a writhing mass of uncertainty.

Violet shook her head. "Most witches and shifters never

know what they could be and what is missing. They bumble through life looking and never finding. So many have been taught to fear the bond because of the past and because of the responsibility to each other."

"Again, something I would've liked to know earlier," Sage muttered.

"And I would've explained it all to you after it was announced, and all of this was dealt with. I didn't think you'd—"

"What? Jump into bed so fast?" Sage lifted one eyebrow. The bond was sealed whether Violet liked it or not. Although only Kirk had come, so maybe it wasn't as complete as it should be.

Kirk shook his head. "You thought Sage would be more wary of me."

"I told him you were a vampire," Violet said.

"But not a witch," Sage said. Would he have been more cautious if he'd known what Kirk truly was, or would he not have cared? "How many know what vampires are?"

Violet shrugged. "Those that bother to learn."

So anyone with an interest in witches and familiars would probably know. His brothers already knew about the vampire in town, his mother knew he was a familiar, and Stone knew who Kirk was. The lid wasn't going to stay on the pot much longer.

But he didn't know how to confront a killer.

"Maybe we should get the cops involved."

"They didn't care twenty years ago; they won't care now." Kirk stared at the headstones and the shortening shadows. "Maybe I shouldn't care." He looked at Violet. "I don't know what happened that night, only that a cougar killed Abby. Maybe it was a mistake and he hasn't killed again." He turned to Sage and added, "Any idiot could've slashed my tires.

There's no reason to think that this is about witches and familiars."

And yet, it probably was. Why had Kirk gotten cold feet all of a sudden? "You think we should do nothing and wait?"

"I think that if it's about my family, then the killer will come to us." Kirk didn't look to thrilled about it. "If fate brought me here, then it's all going to happen anyway so...why push."

Violet stepped back. "If blood is spilled, the Coven will come."

Kirk cracked his knuckles. "I won't be the one spilling blood. I don't need to"

But if the killer attacked as a cougar, there wasn't much skin for Kirk to work with. Sage didn't want his mate risking his life. There had to be a better option. "Wouldn't it be easier to invite Kirk around for dinner?"

"No," Violet and Kirk said together.

"Why?" Sage didn't understand when one meal could solve the problem.

"Because if the killer realizes there's a bond then they might use it against you," Violet said.

"And I'm not ready for your brothers to hate me more than they already do. Also, I'd rather face the killer off home soil. They can come at me in the open."

———

KIRK HOPED he sounded braver than he felt but having been jumped once on the ranch, he had no desire to have it happen a second time. The killer would know too many hiding places, and while there were unaware humans in the town, maybe the killer would think twice about shifting to fight him if there was a risk of being caught. Though the killer hadn't cared when it came to Abby.

He watched as the seer drove away. She hadn't been as helpful as Sage had hoped. Frustration simmered in the shifter's blood and had nowhere to go. Kirk glanced at his hands. He wasn't good enough as he was...Sage wanted to fix him.

Did he want to be fixed? He wasn't even sure what that meant or what it would involve. He knew what it was to be a vampire, not a witch. But if the Coven wanted him dead, that was going to kill Sage and surely they wouldn't do that.

"What now?"

"We get lunch."

Kirk rolled his eyes. "You get lunch." He got to remember what it was like to eat a full meal. If being fixed let him eat again, that would be great.

Eating was another good reason not to have dinner at the ranch; he didn't want them all staring and wondering why he wasn't eating food, or worse, flinching every time he brushed past one of them because they knew something wasn't right. If they knew, they'd accuse him of eating them even if he wasn't. Everyone would pull away or find a reason not to be near him.

If he could be fixed, would that mean he could sit at a family dinner?

Would that be worth it? He'd thought he'd known who and what he was. Now he didn't know anything.

Sage studied him, then turned away and got in the truck.

Kirk did the same. He shut the door harder than he needed to. "What if I can't be fixed? If this is how I am forever...is that going to be good enough?"

"We'll work it out."

"I'm not the kind of witch you were expecting."

"I wasn't expecting anything." Sage started the car and pulled out onto the road.

"But you were hoping that the seer or the Coven would be able to do something."

"Do you want to stay like this? Never able to touch and unable to eat a proper meal?"

Kirk stared out the window. "I don't know. I'm not my magic, and I don't want to be on the Coven's hit list. I didn't become this deliberately." He hadn't even been aware that his magic was being twisted because he didn't know what it should've been.

"I know. I just..." Sage didn't finish. There wasn't really anything he could say.

"It might be best if we don't do anything that might strengthen the bond." Neither of them had expected this. Maybe it wasn't too late to unravel their lives.

"You don't want it?" It wasn't the tone that gave away Sage's hurt but a much deeper current.

"I don't need you to be my familiar to like you. But do I like you because we were drawn together by the bond? Without it would you have even looked at me twice? Would you have looked at my hands, sensed the weirdness around me, and kept your distance?" He sighed. "What's really us and what is magic?"

Sage worried his lower lip between his teeth, looking younger than he was, and more uncertain. After minutes that felt like eons he finally spoke. "I don't think it matters. Why is anyone drawn to anyone else. What is chemistry and lust if not a little magic that smooths the bumps in relationships? Why question the Fates when they throw something good in your lap?"

No one had ever called Kirk good. His grades had been given grudgingly at school as though he didn't deserve them because his mom cleaned the floors. His mentor had called him lazy when he didn't learn magic fast enough or find where the homeless shifters had moved onto. Even Abby had called him a weirdo as she ruffled his hair.

How was this supposed to work when everyone he'd ever loved had died?

He'd been prepared to live alone and celibate—the torture of being a vampire without any of the fun. He wasn't ready to actually have a life, and he had no idea how to include someone else in that life.

Sage parked at the Old Gully Bar and paused keys in hand. "Do you think you were drawn back because of us or because of your sister?"

"I don't know." He wasn't sure if everyone did end up where they were supposed to be, like the seer said. He'd spent time with other teens on the streets and Kirk was damn sure none of them were meant to be there. "Violet should've warned you, and I don't trust her." Sage opened his mouth, but Kirk put his finger on his familiar's lips. "You want to defend her because she's family. How will you feel when the killer does reveal himself? Will you defend him? Or me?"

If Sage wanted to live, he couldn't let Kirk die. But that wasn't a choice.

Sage closed his mouth, his lips brushing Kirk's fingers in a way that was too tantalizing. Kirk already knew the things that mouth could do. He pulled his hand back, but from the way Sage smiled, Kirk knew they'd been thinking something similar.

"Violet did nothing wrong. I don't like that she didn't warn me, but I understand why. I mean, I might have thrown myself at you and ended up at your place eager to be a familiar." He covered Kirk's hand with his own. "Instead I did it because I wanted to be with you."

"That doesn't solve the problem of our lives being linked."

"Sure it does. I'll sleep at the B&B with you."

That wasn't a solution. "What about not strengthening the bond?"

"What about it? I can sleep in the same bed as a man and not have sex."

Kirk shook his head. "You are a terrible liar."

"Well I'm sure I can, I've just never wanted to because that completely misses the point. And when I go to the city, I only have a few days, so I'm not wasting them playing hard to get." He lifted Kirk's hand and kissed his scarred knuckles. "Are you going to eat with me, or do I have to feel like an ass?"

"I'll get something. I can eat, just not much. But it would be nice to see you buy your own meal for a change." Every other time they'd eaten together, Sage had eaten his.

Sage grinned. "Lunch is on me."

He'd be a cheap date.

They got out of the truck, walked into the bar, and took a seat by the windows. The waitress bought menus and for a few minutes Kirk was able to forget about everything else. He could pretend that he was having lunch with his boyfriend.

Were they even that? He had no idea. They'd jumped all the steps that should've been there. What movies did Sage like? Did he have hobbies beyond shifting? What was his favorite food, color, and flavor of ice cream?

"You're feeling very pensive."

Kirk glanced up. "Pensive? I was thinking."

Sage's leg brushed his. "Brooding. Like a *vampire*." He whispered the last word.

"I was not. I don't brood."

"Okay," Sage said with a smile that betrayed his humor. "I'm getting the beef pie. You?"

Kirk scanned the menu looking for something that would be interesting for a few bites, but all he wanted was the man opposite him. "What do you recommend since you'll be finishing it?"

"Sticky ribs."

"Fine." He put down the menu.

"If you don't like ribs, the chicken is good."

"Ribs are fine." Something tickled across his skin and he glanced out the window. Four shifters walked by. While they were all older, he only recognized one by feel. Clay.

Sage followed his gaze. "Hopefully they won't come in."

"My luck isn't that good." The best he could hope for was that they weren't looking for him.

The waitress came over and took their order. By the time they were done, the shifters were inside.

Sage leaned closer. "Any of them?"

"No." They'd already eliminated Clay. Kirk didn't know the names of the others, only that they were getting a drink and having a laugh like they had no troubles. "Who are they?"

"Cousins."

"Names so I can cross them off."

"Check shirt is Heyden, red hair is Jute, Clay you know, and the other one is Ash."

That left Mica, Leif, Jay, and Hunter on the list.

"Maybe they won't notice us."

Kirk stared at Sage. Of course, they'd look over. That's what people did in conversation gaps. They looked around to see what else was going on. Worse they'd probably be able to smell him, and they'd know he wasn't as human as he looked. As if reading Kirk's mind, Clay noticed them. He straightened and wandered over, beer in hand.

Sage bit back a groan but kept his smile in place.

Clay stopped at the table. "How's it going?"

"Great," Sage said, which was about as far from the truth as things could be. The killer was still out there. Their lives were tied together, and the Coven would soon be breathing down Kirk's neck, trying to fix him or kill him.

Kirk assessed Clay; he had the same energy as a man as he did when a cougar. He could feel the other the way he could with all paranormals, but he couldn't sense any more than that. It was only with Sage he could feel the opposing energy of his other form.

Clay's gaze landed on him.

Kirk smiled. "Can I help you?"

"Nah. Just checking that my brother is okay."

"Why wouldn't he be?" The air between them thickened with tension. It crackled on the tip of his tongue and while he could sense it, Kirk couldn't use it or feed on it. His one skill was killing with a touch. What else should he have been able to do if his magic hadn't been corrupted?

"I know what you are."

It was disconcerting that so many knew what vampires were. Or had word gotten around that there was a vampire in town, and they all wanted a look at the freak? "And?"

"Back off, Clay. Kirk's a friend."

Friend. Were they even that without the magic?

"Don't get your tail in a knot. I was just saying hi." Clay took a swig of his beer, studying Kirk. Then turned to his brother and added, "Be careful."

Kirk rolled his eyes. "I want to kiss him not kill him."

That made Clay flinch. That told Kirk more about Clay than he realized. Clay didn't check out all of Sage's boyfriends out of concern; he did it because he didn't like his brother dating men. Clay took a few steps back, and then returned to his friends.

"That was awkward," Sage said.

"He's never liked any of your boyfriends, has he?"

Sage shook his head. "I thought he'd get used to it eventually. Mom and Stone are fine."

There was a big difference between fine and accepting and loving. Most of Kirk's family hadn't cared. It had just been a part of him. But Mom had bigger problems, and Abby had liked discussing attractive guys with him; their tastes had been different. What would his family say now? Mom would be glad he wasn't a danger. Abby would laugh at him for getting tangled with a Madison. Dad, if he'd been well enough to get out of bed, probably would've done more than shout a few hideous comments.

Had Mom hurried him to the end after Kirk came out?

That was something Kirk didn't want to dwell on.

Their meals arrived but their lunch had been spoiled, and Kirk was too aware of the cluster of shifters at the bar who were busy avoiding looking over. He ate a little of his ribs and salad and agreed that they were very nice. Sage tried some and generally tried to make the best of their date being crashed by his older brother and friends.

Sage traced over some of the scars. "Do the symbols mean something?"

"Yeah. They're an energy focus so I can control the flow in and out."

"You said you had a mentor." He paused and Kirk nodded. "He was like you?"

"Yes." Kirk knew where this was going. "In exchange for helping him around the house and running errands he said he'd teach me about magic." He kept his voice soft. "At the time it seemed like a good deal."

It had probably saved his life. He'd already been dangerous to people he touched. He found reasons to turn away from contact because he was starting to hurt his friends and he didn't want to be tossed out of the group when they realized it was Kirk making them tired or ill. He was just like his mother.

"When did you realize it wasn't?"

"What makes you think I did?"

Sage touched Kirk's chest. "Something you carry with you."

He wasn't sure he liked someone else being so close to his feelings, and then having to explain them. But he nodded. "When he carved my knuckles for the first time. At twenty-one, I burned the sigils off my skin. I didn't want to be beholden to him; I wanted to work. I'd finished my high school diploma in secret and had gotten a job as an orderly at the nearby hospital. I wanted more than skulking around the house playing vampire."

Sage rubbed his hand over the scars. "But you went back."

"Yeah. Because I nearly killed a hook up. He carved me up again, but by then I was working fulltime at the hospital. He needed me to stay with him, but I wanted my own life. I should've left completely, but I was too scared to be on my own. I didn't want to hurt anyone. With me around less, I think he got darker. Or maybe I became more suspicious."

"He was killing."

Kirk nodded. "I lied to the seer. I killed one person. My mentor."

Sage leaned back. Kirk missed the lack of contact immediately. But there were no ripples of disgust. Only shock.

The waitress appeared at their table, with a too perky smile. "Can I get you anything else?"

Kirk doubted she had the power to rewind the last five minutes so he could take back the conversation. "I'm good, thanks."

"Can you get us the bill?" When she was gone Sage leaned forward. "It's not a good idea to lie to Violet."

"Why?"

"Because she has a tendency to find out."

"And?" That didn't bother him.

"And you're part of the family now."

Kirk laughed, then smothered it just as fast. Sage was being dead serious. Oh...he had not thought this through. "I'm not a Madison."

"But you are by magic."

A shudder traced down his spine. The shifters at the bar laughed a little too loudly. There were going to be people who didn't like that at all.

CHAPTER THIRTEEN

SAGE TWIRLED his keys around his finger as they made their way to the truck. He barely knew Kirk, and while he trusted the bond and the magic between him. He wasn't sure he trusted the man. Not yet. Which made his attraction and need to touch him all that more confusing. Kirk was right when he'd questioned what was magic and what was them, and there was no answer; if they were meant to be what did it matter?

A little part of him was happy he would be named the next Madison familiar. The rest was concerned about how things would work out when they uncovered who the killer was.

A blur caught the corner of his vision, and he turned as Kirk stumbled and went down with Ash was on top of him. Ash swung at Kirk's head, but Kirk blocked and grasped Ash's hand. Ash froze.

Sage stepped toward them, his heart in his throat, not sure if he was worried that Kirk would hurt Ash or Ash would hurt him. Clay got there first and pulled Ash off. "What the hell, man?"

"What did you do to me?" Ash shook himself like he'd just

fallen in the cold river. "Are you okay with your brother sleeping with this abomination?"

Kirk sat up. "Ever the bully, aren't you Ash?"

He sounded calm but the knots in Sage's stomach weren't his own; they were Kirk's. He didn't like being surrounded by so many cougars. They were in the parking lot behind the bar—not so different to how it had been for Abby.

Ash lunged, fingers curled into fists, and Clay held on.

Sage stepped between them. Kirk was his mate, and he'd protect him no matter what. He wanted the time and the opportunity to see what else they could be. Maybe it didn't matter that magic was the catalyst. "Back off."

The other two, second or third cousins Sage only ever saw every ten years, hung back. But he heard their whispers. They didn't know what Kirk was. Without taking his gaze off Ash, Sage offered Kirk his hand. Kirk didn't get up; he crossed his arms over his knees as though he was at a picnic not sitting on asphalt.

Ash shrugged out of Clay's grip. "Your brother is fucking a vampire."

"And? Sage can sort his own life out," Clay said with a look that suggested he thought otherwise.

"And Sage is standing right here." The words had more snap than he'd intended. Sage crossed his arms, not liking that his sex life was being discussed, but stayed between Ash and Kirk.

"It isn't right," Ash spat. Fury burning in his eyes.

Sage growled. A low warning. He'd seen that look before, though this time Sage wasn't sure if it was because he had a boyfriend, or because the boyfriend was a vampire. Maybe both. Either way, he was done with Ash and his snide comments.

Clay glanced at Sage as though weighing his options, then nodded. "I've checked Kirk out. He's fine."

"Fine?" Ash snarled. "He did something to me. He's not safe. You're a cop. Do something about him."

Clay shrugged. "I'm out of area. And you attacked first. The way I see it, the way most cops would see it, Kirk defended himself. You're still alive, not a scratch on you, so I think we should leave the lovebirds to it."

Sage gritted his teeth, but he could see what defending his boyfriend cost Clay. Maybe he'd misjudged his brother. In another ten years he might welcome Sage's partner instead of tolerating him. "Thanks."

"I'm going to report you to the Coven," Ash said.

Sage tensed. He glanced over his shoulder, but Kirk was smiling.

"You do that." Kirk stood, his eyes bright like amber in sunlight. He dusted off his hands and cracked his knuckles. "Come at me again and I won't just give you a jolt."

Ash stepped forward and Sage put his hand on his cousin's chest. Ash glanced down. "You're choosing *him* over family?" Ash lifted his hands as though innocent as he took a step back. "I should've known. You aren't even one of us."

The word had barely left Ash's mouth before Sage swung a sharp uppercut. Ash wasn't Sage's family. Sage owed him nothing. Kirk was his witch, his mate, and maybe more. Ash wasn't stealing that. The punch connected with Ash's jaw, and he stumbled back unsteady on his feet.

Ash shook off the punch and lifted his hands. "You little shit."

"Enough. Both of you," Clay said. "Sage is family. And you're being dicks."

"That hasn't changed," Kirk muttered.

"I don't even know who you are, vampire."

"Kirk Gracewell. The kid you used to trip up and shove whenever you saw me around school and town."

A flicker of recognition crossed Ash's face, but he shrugged as though the name meant nothing. Clay's eyes narrowed as though he'd caught the slip, too. Now that Kirk had given himself away it would be all over the ranch that he was back and that he was a vampire. There went the seer's hope for secrecy.

"Head home, Ash. I'll get a lift with Sage." Clay gave Sage a pointed look like they weren't done.

Sage wanted to be done. He didn't want to be driving Clay home and getting either a lecture or disapproving glares.

With a few more grumbles, Ash and the other two headed over to the sleek black SUV that had never seen a dirt road before hitting the ranch's driveway. It was only when they'd pulled away that Clay spoke.

"I don't know what's going on, but it would probably be best to tell me."

Sage gave Kirk a warning glance. The seer had said not to tell anyone, and that included his overprotective eldest brother.

Kirk ignored him and stepped closer, and to Clay's credit he didn't flinch back from the vampire. "My sister didn't commit suicide twenty years ago. She was killed by a cougar shifter—a Madison. I want to know who."

Clay stared at him. "Assuming that's true, why did you wait?"

"Fear. I thought I'd moved on but realized I hadn't. I had to come back. I have no living family. One of you took that from me." There was venom in his voice that startled Sage. Kirk had grown up hating Sage's family, and then fearing them.

Could Kirk ever love him?

"You want revenge," Clay said.

"Justice," Kirk countered. "I just want to know who and why and give them the same treatment they gave Abby."

"And you knew this?" Clay asked of Sage.

Sage nodded. "I know it won't make me popular but helping Kirk is the right thing to do." And it felt wrong to be omitting the biggest part of why he'd been roped into helping in the first place. Clay was a cop; he couldn't turn away from this. "One of us is a murderer."

Clay looked at Kirk. "How sure are you?"

"A silver cougar behind the old video store sure. I saw it. If I'd been close enough to see him before he'd shifted, I'd be able to tell who it was. All I know is that it was a man, and his energy tasted like gin and frost-rimmed pebbles."

"There's no identikit for that." Clay raised his eyebrows. "That's why you were at the ranch the other day."

"Yeah."

Clay put his hands on his hips and stared up the sky. "You always brought home the wounded birds, Sage. Always wanting to save everyone." He shook his head. "Twenty-year-old eyewitness testimony with no other evidence is going to be a hard sell."

He might have brought home a couple of injured animals as a child, but this was completely different. "We can't protect a killer."

"If there's a killer."

"I know what I saw," Kirk bit out.

Clay beckoned Sage away from Kirk. "Are you taking his side just because you've fallen into his bed?"

"No. If he were lying, why wouldn't he have already picked one of us out?"

"He could be using you."

"For what? He has a job and a life in the city. You've checked him out. What did you find?"

"Nothing. No record. He finished high school in the city and inherited from the old man he cared for. Aside from being a vampire, he's an upstanding citizen."

"But?"

"But something about him ruffles my fur. You don't feel it?"

"Er...yeah. But I like it." He felt the heat spread over his cheeks and risked a glance at Kirk. He was leaning against Sage's truck as though he didn't have a care in the world.

Clay blew out a breath. "Have you two put together a list of suspects?"

"Yep, and we can cross Ash and friends off."

"How many does that leave you with?"

"Four, I think. Unless I forgot someone. Or we made assumptions that were wrong. Do you want to sit down and do this right?"

"I'm on leave. And I don't work homicides."

"What if he's killed others?"

Clay winced. "Fine. I'll go over the names and your assumptions, then you can take me home. You can have dinner with the family, and we can think of ways to question the suspects without rousing their suspicions."

"Fine."

"Kirk stays here."

Sage couldn't argue with that. The seer had been quite clear that Kirk being on the ranch wouldn't be helpful. With Clay's help they might stand a chance.

There were four names on the list after a conversation with Clay and Kirk over another beer: Hunter, Leif, Jay, and Mica. Clay hadn't liked the look of any of them. While he hadn't said it, Sage could see he wanted to discount all of them straight away simply because he knew them and was friends with them. But twenty years ago was a long time, and even he couldn't remember much about that gathering beyond being able to legally drink.

Sage dropped Kirk at the B&B, and Kirk had vowed to stay indoors. Hopefully in the communal loungeroom where it would be much harder for anyone to come after him.

Sage pulled up to the house and parked in his spot, glad something was going his way. "Do you think Ash has told everyone there's a vampire in town?"

"Probably. He's probably already called the Coven, too. That won't be good for your...your boyfriend."

"Still sticks in your throat, hey."

"I want you to be happy, but a vampire?" Clay managed to look genuinely concerned.

"If he was a prince, you'd still find a reason." Sage looked at his brother. "You don't have to watch over me. You don't have to try and be Dad."

Clay stared straight ahead. "You never had one. I felt bad about that. I knew him, I remember him. Stone barely does and you never stood a chance. I wanted that for you."

"I'm not gay because I didn't have a dad."

Clay gave him a weak smile. "True."

"Just be my brother." Sage offered his hand, and Clay pulled him into an awkward embrace.

"I'll try."

That was about all Sage could ask of anyone.

"You smell different." Clay drew back. His eyebrows pinched together.

Sage shrugged and hoped that he didn't look as guilty as he felt. Was it because of the bond? "I probably just need a shower."

"Maybe." Clay didn't look convinced. "Don't go poking

around, okay? If someone here did kill Abby, they might get pissed if they're found out."

That, Sage hadn't thought of. He'd been so worried about Kirk that he hadn't considered his own position. "I promise I won't say a thing."

He spent what was left of daylight checking on ranch jobs and avoiding most other people—except for a few kids that wanted to help. They did not, in fact, help at all. And a what should've been a quick job became an hour of work, but he didn't mind. For the first time he felt he and Kirk might have a chance. They had help now, people who knew what they were doing.

Violet had been wrong about keeping everything a secret.

After showering and messaging Kirk that he'd come by after dinner, Sage joined the extended family for dinner. Everyone was talking about the vampire in town and what should be done. Sage glanced at Clay and bit his tongue.

Then Ash suggested a vampire hunt. He had a smirk on his face like hunting boyfriends was something fun.

Sage put down his fork. "This isn't the Middle Ages. We can't go around hunting people."

"You don't get an opinion, traitor." Ash pointed his table knife at him. "In fact, you shouldn't even be sitting at this table."

"Enough." Mom stood. "You don't get to decide who is good enough to part of this family. Your dad tried that once."

Sage drew in a breath, expecting Ash and Mica to arc up about how the ranch should be theirs, but his cousins merely looked like resentful thunderclouds. They'd find a way to spend their anger. Hopefully they'd burn it off with a shift—not a vampire hunt.

Ash shrugged. "Fine. We'll let the Coven deal with it, Seer?"

Violet dabbed her lips with a napkin and without looking at Sage said in a voice that was all honey. "Yes. I'm sure you've already called without checking what the other elders and I have discussed."

Ouch.

Everyone was suddenly really busy cutting their food and eating.

"No time to waste," Ash said. "Sage has already been corrupted."

"Oh, for crying out loud." Sage put down his cutlery. Stone tried to stop him from standing, but Sage was done. "Yes, I am dating the vampire." He didn't correct anyone and reveal that meant Kirk was a witch. "Any more questions?"

Apparently, there were. Everything from they aren't real, to wasn't that dangerous, to why and who was he. Kirk's name made a few people pause as if it were vaguely something familiar. Clay watched those people on the list the way he did when he was hunting as a cougar. When he pounced, no one would know until it was too late. It was nice to have Clay on his side instead of feeling like his brother existed only to make his life difficult.

"So, we are clear. No hunting of the vampire," Violet said, taking the role of leader since she was the seer.

"Should be no dating of the vampire," Ash muttered.

"We do not run other paranormals out of town. We never have and we never will. When the Coven investigator that you have called arrives this will all be sorted," Violet continued as though Ash hadn't interrupted.

And what if the investigator decided that Kirk was too broken and should die? That would mean Sage would die, too. Or would the Coven try to break the bond first? It wasn't very strong. They'd barely done anything, but that could easily be rectified.

He didn't want to lose his mate; they'd only just found each other. And he'd gotten used to the idea far too quickly.

There were grumbles that vampires were dangerous and there was a reason they were supposed to be extinct. But most of the shifters weren't here to stir up trouble; they were here to catch up with family. That didn't stop Sage from receiving looks that ran the spectrum from smirks to pity to hostility.

How would they all feel when it was announced he was a familiar and that Kirk was a witch?

He glanced at Violet, wishing she'd break protocol and just say something now. But then his gaze drifted to the four suspects and he understood, in his bones, why she wouldn't tell until the killer was outed. At least two of the suspects wouldn't give a damn if Sage died; his incidental death might even make the idea of hunting Kirk more appealing.

Secrecy was still in his favor.

Clay caught his eye and shook his head. *Nothing yet.*

Sage finished his meal, then went outside to bathe in the moonlight. There wasn't much of it. He was going to head back into town, but he'd be up early to get back here and do his jobs.

And when Kirk went back to the city? Would weekends be enough? How long until it became every second weekend? Or monthly?

Stone appeared next to him. "You okay?"

"Yeah. I'm sure it would've been worse if I'd been dating a wolf shifter." All the jokes about cats and dogs would soon follow. "You didn't tell the truth about vampires."

The weight of the secret grew heavier with each breath. It would come out before he was ready. How many at dinner knew that a vampire was a witch, but had said nothing? Did they suspect? His chest became tight. He wanted the hunt for the killer over so he could learn how to breathe again. But when it was over what would happen? Was there more than murder between them?

"Neither did you. I didn't think it would be wise. People might jump to other assumptions." Stone studied him. "Would they be correct?"

Sage held his gaze then gave a single nod. There was no point in hiding it from Stone, and Stone would never tell a soul.

Stone hugged him and whispered in his ear, "Well done. You need to be extremely careful, buddy."

"When did you know?"

"About you or him?"

"Both."

"I know what a vampire is, the rest wasn't hard to figure out." He glanced away and sighed. "I work for the Coven."

Sage drew back and stared at his brother. For how long had Stone carried that secret? Was he watching everyone and reporting? "What?"

"I'm not an investigator, but they're sending one."

"Should I worry?"

"I don't know. Go and enjoy your night. You are going back into town, right?"

Sage studied the ground. "I was just waiting around a bit to be less obvious."

"I think that horse has well and truly bolted."

True. Everyone knew so why bother hiding it. "I'll be back at dawn."

"It's fine. I've almost got my kids convinced that alpacas aren't terrifying hell-beasts." He clapped Sage on the arm. "Get out of here."

"Thanks." He jogged down the steps, and rounded the corner of the house, stepping into the shadows. His mind was already on what it would be like to spend the night with Kirk.

Screw caution; he wanted to strengthen the bond between them.

A red sports car was blocking the way. He went to squeeze past.

"Where you going?" a man said.

Sage glanced behind. Pain rung through the side of his head and the ground raced toward him.

CHAPTER FOURTEEN

KIRK SAT in the lounge room reading a book, but the other man in the room wanted to talk even though Kirk had made it clear he didn't, so he retreated to his room. His book now lay unread on the bedside table as a headache throbbed behind his eyes. He hadn't had a headache in a long time—not since he was training and getting used to absorbing energy instead of food.

That should've been an indication that something was wrong with what he was learning, but he didn't know anything about magic or what he was. He'd been scared and needing help and a home, and so he looked past every oddity until he was forced to confront the truth.

If he'd been smarter and braver, he'd have challenged his mentor earlier.

And he would've been killed.

He'd almost died anyway. It had taken him a week to recover and he'd had to fake being okay because everyone had questions about how the old man had died. Nothing had traced back to him, though he'd been terrified the Coven would hear of the mysterious death and investigate.

In the end Kirk was told the old man's heart had given out. Then he was told he was the sole recipient in the will. He hadn't needed to fake his surprise.

He put his arm over his eyes, not wanting any light to intrude. Maybe he should go back out and feed off the man in the lounge to see if that got rid of the pounding in his skull. But the idea of getting up was too much.

If the Coven turned up now, what determination would they make? Would they help him find Abby's killer? Or would they only care that a witch had turned into a magically stunted vampire?

He hated killing.

His old promise to find out who murdered his sister and make them pay had been made in rush and anger and fear. He'd be happy to hand the killer to the Coven and be done. He didn't need revenge like he thought he did. But would handing the killer over fulfill his vow to Abby?

He sighed. Abby was dead; nothing would change that. All he wanted was closure.

And Sage.

A smile formed but was quickly erased by a wave of dizziness. He tried to sit up and struggled. Something was wrong... but not wrong with him. His life was connected to Sage and Sage was in trouble.

He sat on the edge of the bed and gripped the mattress. With slow deep breaths he untangled what *he* felt and put aside the pain and confusion that weren't his. The headache receded to a throb in his temple. But the urgency to get to Sage increased, pulsing in his blood.

Kirk pulled on his boots, put the room key in his pocket, and grabbed his phone. He deliberated sending Sage a message but opted not to; he didn't want to alert the person hurting Sage that he was coming. But he wanted to let Sage knew he was on his way. He tried to push reassuring thoughts through their connection, the same delicate spider web of energy that he'd follow to find Sage.

While Sage had warned Kirk that he could be in danger, Sage had thought himself safe. And Sage should've been. Except he was at home...with the killer.

Kirk left the B&B. The streetlights cast puddles of light in another wise inky night. The moon was a slice of a promise. His mentor liked to go out on nights like this. They were made for hunting, for predators to find prey. Kirk shuddered and shoved his hands in his pocket, not sure which one he was.

He paused at the gate and let the tug in his gut choose his direction, trusting it to lead him to Sage. Then he started walking. He kept an even, busy pace through the town where people were still having dinner or drinking in the bar, but once out of the town center he jogged, wishing he had his bike and not sure he'd be in time, silently vowing to take on every cougar that got in his way.

If Sage died, Kirk would spend what time he had left making them all suffer.

———

SAGE'S HEAD hurt and he was groggy, and even when lying down in the dark the world swam. He tried to move to take the pressure off his shoulder and couldn't. Panic kicked in, making his heart beat faster and his head pound harder.

Where was he?

He couldn't stretch out; his hands were tied behind his back. For a few seconds he gave into the fear before he realized it wasn't helping. He forced several slow breaths. After that it took less than five seconds to figure out he was in the trunk of a car.

He ran through the list of suspects. Mica, Leif, Hunter and Jay. He'd been near Mica's red sports car when attacked. So, the odds were good that he was in Mica's car...the killer's car.

For several seconds he lay there not sure what to do with that information. Not a lot while he was trapped and didn't know where he was. He was fairly sure he didn't have his phone on him. And he was tied up. He needed to get out of the ropes.

Could he shift?

He considered it for a heartbeat. He'd be tangled in clothes, and the rope might slip off and while he still thought as a man even when it the cougar body his senses were different, and the cat would not be as calm in the trunk. Though his calm as a man was whisker thin.

He wriggled until his back was pressed to the metal of the trunk behind him and he ran his fingers over the surface trying to work out which way he was facing, then turned again feeling for anything that would help him.

He'd always thought this was a stupid car. Not enough room to swing a cat in the trunk. The more he moved, the hotter he became and the harder it was to breathe.

Beneath his fear was something else. A need to go faster.

Kirk was coming for him.

———

WITH THE STREETLIGHTS left behind in town, Kirk's eyes adjusted to the night and the open space where sky touched land in a glittering array of stars. He'd never appreciated the beauty until he'd been unable to find it in the city. The gnawing in his gut led him on, and he jogged at a steady pace, knowing he could keep it up all night—longer if he found someone to feed on. It was a pity the cattle in the fields that lined the road were of no use to him.

Desperation clawed through him. His and Sage's. He had the feeling of being confined and unable to breathe even though there was only sky and silence out here. Wherever Sage was, he was trapped.

His phone buzzed with a message. He didn't pause as he read it.

Heading into town now.

Kirk stopped and stared at his phone. What he saw on the screen was at odds with what he felt. Was he wrong? He stood still, miles out of town in the middle of nowhere on what he'd thought was a rescue. He'd trusted the bond and it was wrong. Or he was wrong about the feelings swamping him? Probably the latter.

What did he know about magic and familiars?

He glanced back toward the town, then up the road toward where the ranch was.

His gut wanted him to keep going to Sage. Ignoring the pull wouldn't make it go away. If he met Sage on the road, they could laugh about it later. Decision made, he resumed jogging.

Another mile passed.

Headlights cut through the night.

Kirk glanced away so as not to lose his night vision and moved to the side of the road. The truck was the same golden color as Sage's. He watched as it drew closer until he could be sure, then stepped out and waved it down.

He was an idiot. He should've stayed in bed and waited for Sage to arrive.

And the fear and panic and pain?

Maybe Sage had been playing games with some other cougars. Maybe when he shifted, Kirk felt that change. There were so many questions.

The truck slowed, close enough now that he could feel the energy of the man inside. He expected cinnamon.

He tasted icy pebbles and bitterness.

Without pausing to look in the dark cab, Kirk ran. Not to town, but toward Sage. Sage was trapped and afraid. The truck stopped and turned. Kirk pushed harder, knowing he wasn't going to reach Sage. He was going to have to stop and fight or take his chances with the cattle.

The truck approached. Kirk got off the road, heading to the fence, knowing it would be electrified.

The first shot went wide.

The second hit his back.

He stumbled and went down, heat and pain tearing through his body. Blood spilled out of his chest and he couldn't quite catch his breath.

The truck stopped, and the man got out, rifle in hand. "Kind of my cousin to keep one in his truck."

Kirk kept his hand on the wound, even though he knew pressure wouldn't do much when there was a hole all the way through him. Blood poured through his fingers. He was prolonging the inevitable. How much would he need to feed, so he wouldn't die?

"What do you want?" Kirk rasped out.

"A witch."

"I'm a vampire." Kirk smiled, sure he could taste blood in his mouth.

The man levelled the rifle at Kirk. "Don't be dumb. Your family has a long history of being witches. Except for your bitch sister."

Kirk's lips curled into a snarl. "You killed her."

He needed to get a hand on the shifter. Skin to skin to take some of his life.

"She didn't want to be my witch. And she was very rude about it."

"You didn't have to kill her." Abby would have joked about the idiot who'd thought she was a witch.

"Don't tell me what do to." He fired a shot that hissed passed Kirk's head.

Which cousin was this? There were only four on the list. Hunter, Jay, Mica and Leif. "What do you want?"

"You're going to be my witch, and I'm going to reclaim the ranch from Sage. I know you've been banging him, but power is better than sex, and I know from the old seer that I was supposed to get a witch. I was meant to be a familiar. She died without telling me who."

"Did you kill the seer?"

The man smiled. "I was a touch too persuasive. Violet...she says nothing to no one. I don't think she has the gift."

Kirk shook his head, blood trickling over his lip. "You can't force the bond."

"That's not true. Witches used to force shifters. They had a spell to keep us trapped as animals, too. It wasn't that hard to find the spells; all we need is some blood."

There was no way he was getting tied to this man. But he didn't want to reveal that he already had a familiar either.

"If we're bound, you'll die if I do."

"You aren't as stupid as you look. I'm not going to let you die. Your first meal is all trussed up and waiting for you."

Kirk's heart stuttered in realization. "Sage."

"I don't want your loyalties mixed, so it seemed appropriate for you to eat your soon to be ex."

"And if I refuse?"

The man levelled the gun at him. "You aren't in a position to say no."

There was always a no. The consequences may not be ideal, but it was still an option. "What do I get out of this?"

"To live."

"As your captive witch."

"Would you rather die?"

"Maybe."

"You're just like your sister, thinking you're so much better than us. You're witch scum. Cleaner's kids. You should be thanking me for even offering this to you."

"How many other witches have you offered this chance of a lifetime to?"

The man smiled, cold and confident. "I've had two other witches, but they burned out within five years." The spell could bind but the bond was imperfect. Damaging. Kirk had seen his mentor try and fail. The man sniffed. "You're different. I can sense it."

Yeah, he already had a shifter. A lover. They were more than witch and familiar. This man wanted power, but he didn't want to share it. Kirk's hand was sticky with blood and he shivered, unable to keep the cold from invading as his life slid between his fingers.

He was going into shock. He needed to feed before he passed out and couldn't.

"Fine. Let's do this." He gathered up everything he had left, ready to shock the shifter into submission so Kirk could feed at leisure.

"No tricks."

Kirk took his hand off his wound. His palm was sticky and dark. "If I pass out from blood loss, I'll be no good to you."

The man pulled a piece of paper out of his pocket and tossed it on the ground. "Read it and be ready to say the words to cast the spell. You are the witch after all."

Kirk picked up the paper and read through the spell. He'd

never done any kind of casting and wouldn't have a clue how to start. But he felt the power in the words in the rhyme and rhythm, and he didn't like the taste of aniseed they left in his mouth.

The man cut his fingertip. "This is a blood binding. Put out your hand. And do your thing."

Kirk glanced up at him. He held the rifle, and even if he couldn't shoot accurately with one hand, he only needed to get lucky once for this to be over.

The man grinned. "And no trying to take my gun."

"Can you put it down? It the interest of trust and this new working relationship?"

"No. There is no trust. You serve me, witch, or you die."

Kirk nodded as though beaten and was agreeing.

"If you do this right, I might let you have a taste of my blood."

Kirk managed not to pull a face. "Thanks. That won't be enough for me to heal, though."

"So the quicker you do this, the sooner you can bite Sage."

This idiot actually thought he drank blood. "Won't the rest of the family be pissed about that?"

"Don't worry about that; I've got it all figured out. This isn't my first witch hunting. I wasn't planning on finding a witch at the gathering, but when I heard you were in town, I knew it was meant to be." He held out his bloodied finger.

Kirk offered his hand. Their skin connected with a jolt like he'd stuck his finger in a power point. The man dropped to the ground as Kirk grasped the man's finger and didn't let go. He stole his life, taking what he needed to survive.

The sharp cold in his mouth made him want to gag, but he had to stop the bleeding. After a few minutes, it slowed. The wound was hot, the tissue knitted with a twisting pain that left him gasping. Finally, he stood, his legs as soft as the deflated tires on his bike.

He made it to the truck and held onto the side, leaving bloody smears on the paint. He needed to get to Sage...but he couldn't leave the man here. He'd flee and kill again. He wouldn't stop catching witches.

"Fuck." With a wrench of will, he turned around and went back to the man.

The man stirred when he saw Kirk and lifted the rifle. The shot tore through Kirk's shoulder and he landed on his ass.

The man got up, and Kirk lunged for his legs and got a finger under his jeans. The man slammed but butt of the rifle down on the fresh wound. Kirk screamed but didn't let go. He tore into the man's life like a starving beast taking his fill, and then more. The man collapsed, and Kirk took a little extra to make sure he stayed down.

For several breaths all he could do was lie on the side of the road next to the shifter and wait for the dizziness to pass as his broken body mended. He wasn't sure which was worse: being shot or the healing after.

———

SAGE COULDN'T BREATHE. Pain bloomed in his chest, and he curled up unable to do anything but wallow in the hot agony. Just as he caught his breath, another spear of pain went through his shoulder.

But it wasn't his pain.

That thought didn't lessen the heat or the sensation that he was sliding down a dark well with nothing to grab onto. Dizziness overtook him and he wasn't sure which way was up.

He reached out to Kirk. Whatever was happening to him, Sage was getting a taste of and it was nothing good. That warning that their lives were tied together returned. If Mica had Kirk, then they were both damned.

The darkness wanted to swallow him. It dragged him down. Somewhere in there, Kirk flailed and fought, trying to find something to hold onto. Sage tried to reach out to him. He didn't know if he was doing anything more than scowling, but he had to do something.

Take my hand. He offered it metaphorically.

For a moment there was nothing, then he felt as though Kirk was lying next to him, wounded and in pain. *I'll drain you.*

You can't. This is our shared life. If you die, we both die.

Then Kirk was inside his mind, and he wasn't all darkness and sharp edges the way Sage had thought a vampire would be. He was bourbon on ice and fluffy sweet pancakes.

And even though they weren't touching, there was that jolt as Kirk took a little of his life and energy. Sage took some of the pain in return. They had to share because Kirk couldn't feed on him.

Sage squeezed his eyes closed, unable to do more than concentrate on breathing, but knowing he had to move and that the pain wasn't real for him. Yet.

He had to save Kirk.

But he had to free himself first.

Sage tried to work the knot lose, but the rope was too tight. If he could get his hands around the front...

In the small, dark space he struggled. He sweated, and cursed, and bled as the rope cut into his skin. But he didn't care. When he finally had his hands in front of him, he used his teeth to undo the knot. Then with his hands free, he rolled over and searched for the boot release. His fingers grazed something that could be a catch. He gave it a pull and the trunk sprung open.

The house wasn't that far away. The car had been moved to

be closer to the stables were no one would come at night. He hadn't been taken anywhere.

"Help." His voice was like a kitten's.

He struggled to climb out, stumbling and falling on the ground like he had no bones in his legs. Kirk was taking what he needed to survive.

Sage crawled over the grass and dirt toward the porch, like he was drunk. The pebbles bit into his hands and knees, but he didn't dare stop.

"Help," he whispered again unable to speak louder.

Where was everyone? The lights were all off. They were probably sleeping, unaware that Mica had gone vampire hunting.

Sage crawled up the stairs and onto the porch, almost to the door. But when he fell again, he couldn't get up.

———

KIRK DRAGGED the still unconscious man to the truck. Something newly mended inside of Kirk tore, and he started bleeding again. Pain ricocheted through his body. Every breath hurt. Lifting the man into the tray left him weak and panting.

The bond to Sage was all the kept him going. As much as he wanted to hold on, he let go. Sage was as weak as him. And neither of them was safe.

He staggered to the front and got in. It had been a long time since he'd driven a car, longer since he'd driven a stick. He touched the steering wheel aware he was making a mess of the cab. He started the truck, ground into first, and got going. Every bump in the road jostled his wounds. And he fought to stay alert without drawing on the bond between them while trusting it to lead him to Sage.

I'm coming.

CHAPTER FIFTEEN

KIRK SWUNG the truck into the driveway to the ranch. Sage was at home...so why was he hurt? For a heartbeat, Kirk doubted the connection. None of this made sense. Unless Sage's family had turned against him.

He remembered Sage saying he wasn't really a Madison. Maybe being involved with a vampire was too much. Or maybe someone had found out about the bond. All Kirk knew was that if they were together, it would be all right.

He pulled up in front of the house. The headlights lit up the porch and the body of a man.

Sage.

He pressed the horn of the truck, hoping to wake someone, then fell more than got out of the cab, tripping his way to the steps and landing next to the fallen shifter. Sage's heartbeat was soft, his eyes closed and his skin pale.

Kirk had taken too much, and he had nothing to spare to give back to him.

If he took more from the man in the tray of truck...it wouldn't be enough. And he didn't have the strength to get over there, nor did he want to kill a Madison while on their land.

Blood dripped onto the porch. His life, his energy, leaving a drop at a time.

He lay down and pulled Sage close, kissed his cheek, and hoped someone friendly would find them before he ran out of blood.

———

IT WAS the jostling that dragged Sage out of the darkness. Every breath hurt, but he knew it was an echo and not his pain. But he couldn't stop it. He tried to reach for Kirk with his mind but couldn't grab hold. Every time he got close, Kirk melted away like a shadow. Like he didn't want to be touched.

Voices intruded, and Sage was lifted.

He struggled weakly, not wanting to end up back in the trunk of the sports car. "No."

His eyes flickered open, and lights dazzled him. He blinked to clear his vision, still struggling.

"It's okay. We've got you," Stone said as he helped carry Sage upstairs.

Sage relaxed, no longer fighting the people holding him, and closed his eyes. "Kirk." He needed Kirk. Where was he? Was he dying? Were *they* dying?

"We've got him, too."

Sage was placed on a bed. His from the scent. The room was dark, and he opened his eyes, looking for Kirk. He wasn't there. He tried to sit up but didn't have the strength. "Where's Kirk?"

His head still hurt, his chest was collapsing, and he felt like he'd been runover and then been forced to run ten miles.

Stone pushed him back onto the bed. "You need to rest."

Sage grabbed his brother's hand. He didn't care about Violet's desire for caution anymore. "I want my witch."

Stone stared at him. "Are you sure that's a good idea?"

Fresh fear shot through Sage. "What have you done to him?"

"Nothing. We were going to question him about all the blood."

Sage glanced down. There was blood all over him. "It's not mine." It was Kirk's. This was worse than he thought. "If he dies..."

"I know." Stone left the room.

Sage wanted to follow, but he didn't have the strength and he was chilled to the bone. He didn't know how long he'd been lying outside, but he knew when Kirk had reached him. That meant he wasn't far away.

His mother rushed in wearing her dressing gown. "I know I shouldn't have gone prowling with them. I should've been here." She sat on the bed and took his hand.

They'd all shifted and gone out, assuming Sage was with Kirk and making it easy for Mica to disappear, too. "I'm fine."

"Are you?" She touched his face, then his head where it hurt, and her fingers came away bloodied.

"I will be. Mica needs to be found." He needed to be stopped. "He did this."

Clay carried Kirk in, slung over his shoulder like a sack of grain. Mom got up so Kirk could be laid down. They'd taken off his jacket and shirt. The bullet wounds in his chest and shoulder still wept.

Clay shook his head. "This is bad."

Mom pressed her lips together. "Kirk needs to feed. He's an energy witch." She put her hand on Kirk's shoulder, just above the wound. She frowned. "I don't think he can while he's unconscious."

Sage put his hand on Kirk's skin, but there was no familiar tingle. Kirk wasn't responding when Sage reached out with his mind either. Maybe he'd imagined that. But he could feel Kirk's hunger and pain. Maybe Kirk thought he was protecting everyone by retreating. "He's hungry. Maybe he doesn't want to hurt anyone."

"That's very noble," Mom said.

"And stupid," Clay added.

She shot Clay a look. "Get some other volunteers. He might kill one of us, but he can't kill all of us."

"We could take him to hospital," Clay said.

Mom shook her head. "They'd stitch the wounds, but they can't heal the rest. We need to do this. We need a witch on the ranch. He's not just Sage's, he's ours. He's family now."

For a moment, Sage thought Clay was going to argue. Then he turned and left the room.

Sage watched his brother's retreating back. "He's not happy."

She shook her head. "He's practical, and he's never been a big believer in magic and such. Never wanted to learn about being a familiar."

"Mica killed Kirk's sister. He's probably the one who shot Kirk." His voice broke. He didn't have room for anger; he was too full of grief and fear. He and Kirk only just met. They hadn't even explored the magic or what could be between them. Kirk hadn't stirred since being laid down. If not for the small rise of his chest with every slow breath and the fresh trickle of blood, it would be easy to believe he was already dead.

Clay returned with Stone and a few other cousins—not Ash or Mica. No one was wearing shoes and some only had pants on, fresh from shifting with wild eyes and high energy. Even Violet looked disheveled as though she'd been interrupted.

Violet brushed her hand over Kirk's forehead. "You'll need to break through the barrier he's put up."

"I'll try." Sage wished it would be as easy as she made it sound.

Everyone stared at him like he knew what to do. He didn't have a clue; this was all new to him. They'd tested the bond in the worst possible way, but it had worked; he was almost sure he hadn't imagined the connection.

Sage lied down and hooked his fingers around Kirk's in the tiniest of hand holds. There were too many eyes on him and Kirk. He could only imagine what they were thinking, wondering. The scrutiny made his cheeks burn.

"Put your hand on his skin," Violet said to the others. "The worst that will happen is you'll be tired for a day, but it won't be permanent."

"Are you sure?" someone asked.

"It'll be a whole lot less permanent than both of them dying," Sage's mom snapped.

"We're ready, Sage," Violet said softly.

What if this didn't work and he couldn't make Kirk realize that it was safe? Would he get better on his own eventually or weaken and die? Sage wasn't ready to die, so Kirk couldn't either.

He exhaled and let his mind reach for his witch, following the silky bond between them. Was it thicker today that it had been last night?

Kirk, everyone is here to help.

Was he talking to himself or was Kirk hearing him? He wasn't quite sure, but he didn't know what else to do.

You need to feed. I need you to feed. I don't want to lose you.

He didn't try to mask the fear that bubbled up. He'd only just found Kirk, and while he didn't know if it was forever, he knew they'd always have a connection. That had to mean something.

Kirk?

———

THE NEED TO feed clawed inside of Kirk. He'd never been this hungry. It hurt like something wanted to climb out of his skin, and it terrified him. He couldn't let his twisted magic hurt Sage's family, and Kirk knew if he let go for just a moment there would be death.

Their hands pressed against his skin. It would be so easy to open himself up and drown in their life. But he if opened up, even just a crack, it would be all over. They'd hate him and fear him, and Sage would look at him with disgust. The bond between them had given him the ability to shut himself off from everyone—a skill he wished he'd learned a long time ago.

Sage's cougar prowled around him, pleading to be let in.

He'd been wrong about not being able to feed on Sage. He could, but it was different. Energy flowed through the bond. He could give to Sage—something he'd never been able to do with anyone. But he could also take, and Sage needed what he had left.

I don't want to hurt you, and I might.

It would be best if he just sank deeper into himself. Not dead but not alive.

A magical coma which would only end when Sage died.

Sage headbutted against the barrier and purred loud enough to shake the foundations. *I want you alive.*

Kirk wished he'd never come to Madison Gully. If he hadn't, Sage's life never would've never gotten tangled with his. But then he'd never have learned it was Mica who killed Abby.

And she wasn't the only one. If he did nothing, Kirk knew Mica would kill again.

Stop being scared of what you are. Embrace it, Sage shouted in Kirk's head.

The pressure of the Madison's fingers reached into him like they could force him to feed. The throb of their energy was so close. All he had to do was drop his guard and he could stop hurting.

He was a vampire. Some kind of witch. And he had a familiar.

And he was surrounded by people who knew what he was and didn't hate him or fear him. The old fear of being discovered was replace with a new one. That he'd lose the love he'd just found if he didn't fight.

Sage snarled and leaped for the barrier.

Kirk brought it down. The jolt took his breath. Fur brushed skin. An array of tastes filled his mind too many for him to separate, but he took a little from all. His body healed with hot, fresh pain. As he grew stronger, he pushed some of the energy to Sage.

I love you. He needed Sage to know that, no matter what happened.

Purring filled his body. *I love you, too.*

When the heat faded, he pushed back so those touching him felt the static and took their hands away. It would be too easy to feast and drain them all.

As expected, everyone stopped touching him. That they'd willingly offered themselves...no one had ever done that for him. The only person left touching him was Sage, their fingers linked together. He opened his eyes, not sure what he'd find. But only concerned faces stared down.

"Did you see the way the skin mended?" A woman pointed at Kirk's chest. "It just..."

"Grew," someone else finished. They were staring at him.

"That's what healers do," Violet said.

But he wasn't a healer. He could only do that to himself. And maybe Sage.

"Thank you." His voice was rough. Though they probably hadn't actually done it for him. He glanced at the man next to him; Sage looked so much better than he had when Kirk found him lying on the porch.

The others started to leave.

Kirk forced himself up. "Mica is in the back of Sage's truck. He's been binding witches and killing them. He wanted to bind me." Sage's family frowned and stared at him. Did anyone believe him? "Mica wants a witch and to take over the ranch."

Clay said, "I'll go. Stone?"

"I'll update the Coven." Stone pulled out his phone as he walked away.

Kirk swung his legs off the bed.

"You should rest," Sage's mom said. He'd felt her worry and sensed her connection to her sons.

"Mica's dangerous. I came back here to stop him." He'd found Abby's killer and uncovered something worse.

"I'm not letting you go alone," Sage said.

"You've found him and stopped him." Violet stood in the doorway like she was going to stop them. "Leave the rest to Clay and Stone."

"If I wanted to kill him, I'd have done it before bringing him here." Kirk hoped he wouldn't regret leaving Mica alive.

A howl of anguish cut through the house. "Where is he? I'll kill him."

Violet turned, revealing Ash in the hallway.

"Let me through," Ash snarled.

Kirk stood and cracked his knuckles, ready to fight again

even though his wounds had only just healed and all he wanted to do was be with Sage. "Mica shot me three times."

"What did you do to him first?" Ash stepped forward, but Violet put a hand on his chest.

"It's a Coven matter now. Mica has been binding witches. He killed Abby Gracewell, and attacked Kirk and his familiar, Sage."

Ash frowned. "No. He wouldn't do those things." His gaze landed on Kirk and spat, "This is the vampire's doing."

Kirk felt Sage move next to him, then take his hand.

Ash's gaze dropped to the floor. "Familiar." He stepped back and shook his head. "Violet, don't do this. Please, I'll take Mica with me and we'll never come back."

"No, you won't. You are both banished. But Sage and Kirk have the right to pack justice."

Kirk didn't know what that was, but he didn't think it would win him any favors. "How about we leave it to the Coven. That's what you wanted wasn't it, Ash?"

Ash looked like a man who'd found maggots in his steak. "It wasn't meant to be this way. We just wanted our share of the ranch."

"Your father wanted out, and Mom paid him. You have no share," Sage snarled. "Mica would've killed me and bound Kirk. How many more would he have killed to get what he wanted? Clay, Stone, Mom? Violet?" Sage stepped forward. "Get out of the house. You can stay on the property until the Coven investigator arrives, then I want you gone."

"You're not even a Madison. Who are you to give me orders?"

"Back down, Ash." Violet's voice was steel. "Go and sit with Mica. I'm sure Stone and Clay will have made him comfortable."

Ash pointed at Kirk and Sage. "This isn't over."

It was only after Ash stomped away that Kirk realized his heart was beating too hard and fast.

Next to him, Sage sighed. "Will he make trouble?"

"He's angry and confused. Come daylight, we will see." She considered them both for a moment. "Enough blood has been spilled. Thank you for entrusting this to the Coven. That couldn't have been easy."

Kirk shook his head. What else could he have done?

"I'd have liked to rip Mica's throat out," Sage admitted. "But I think Kirk is right and the Coven should deal with him."

Violet gave a single nod. "Maybe we can all heal now the splinter has been found and removed."

"How much did you see?" Kirk asked. Had she seen him get shot? What could've been avoided by knowing more?

"Not enough to stop what happened." She stepped out of the bedroom and shut the door, leaving them in the silvery moonlight slipping through the open curtains.

"I'm not tired." All the energy he'd taken from the shifters was buzzing in his veins. Maybe he'd taken too much, or maybe feeding on shifters left him feeling jittery. Or that was the after effect of nearly dying?

"Me either. Though I should be. And you almost died."

Kirk stared at the carpet. "Yes, but I figured out how to shut you out. I knew I could put myself into a coma."

"Then how would you wake?"

"I don't know. Maybe I wouldn't have." He glanced up. "Your family doesn't hate me?"

Sage pulled Kirk into his arms. "No. I thought I'd lost you. Don't shut me out."

"I don't want to hurt you, and I don't know how this works."

"Neither do I but we'll figure it out together." Sage placed a soft kiss on his lips. "A shower might be a good place to start."

"Yeah." His skin was sticky with blood. The scars beneath were new and pink. "But what about Mica and Ash? They know about the bond and could use it against you."

"My brother's will make sure they don't make any trouble." Sage leaned into him and breathed, "In the meantime we should finish cementing the bond and become as strong as possible."

"What are you suggesting?" But he could already feel the desire in Sage rising, thick and sweet like syrup.

———

SAGE LED Kirk to the bathroom, the hallway fortunately empty. He should be with his brothers, but he didn't want to be anywhere else than by Kirk's side. Kirk followed Sage into the bathroom and Sage shut the door behind them, pinning his mate to the door.

"So...this time we can take our clothes off." He kissed Kirk, slowly not afraid of what might happen. It was there, thrumming between them.

Kirk's hand slid under Sage's T-shirt and over his abs. "But your family...won't they hear?"

"They aren't stupid. They'll be downstairs having tea, or maybe sitting outside. We know how to give each other space."

Kirk glanced away, his fingers knotting around the cloth. "How will this work?"

"I'm hoping you'll stay...that you want to stay. That this will be your home." He pressed his forehead to Kirk's. "But if you don't want to, we can figure things out."

"I don't know if I belong here."

"You do." He cupped Kirk's face. "You're my mate, and my family will accept that...has accepted it." He smiled. "They gave you a little of their lives. If that's not acceptance I don't know what is."

Kirk nodded. "You aren't worried the Coven will drag me away?"

"Nope." Maybe just a little, but that wasn't something he needed to share. He'd fight to keep hold of Kirk. "It was fated to be, so therefore it has to work out."

"You really believe that?"

Sage looked into his witch's amber eyes. "With all my heart."

Kirk gave him a small smile then nodded. "Fate certainly dragged me back here, and I'm glad it was for more than revenge."

"So am I." He pulled off his own T-shirt since Kirk was taking too long. "They won't give us all night."

That was all the invitation Kirk needed to help get the rest of Sage's clothes off, and then his own. Nerves radiated off him. His skin was smeared with blood and his chest and shoulder bore shiny new pink scars. Sage had come too close to losing him.

Sage reached out and ran his palm up Kirk's arm before pulling him close again so he could steal his breath.

"It's been a long time."

"I know. And we've got the rest of our lives...but I really want you to fuck me." Sage stepped back and opened the bathroom vanity. Beneath the sink was the lube. He was usually the only person who used this bathroom. With others in the house, he'd pushed his things to the back and hoped no one would say anything. He almost grabbed condoms but didn't bother. He didn't want anything between them.

He handed the lube to Kirk, who looked like he'd been handed a live grenade. "It's been a really long time. What if I do it wrong and hurt you?"

"You won't, but if you do you'll feel it and you can heal me." He put his hand over Kirk's. "I trust you. Am I rushing you?"

Did Kirk not want to fuck him? It must have shown on his face.

"No. I want you." Kirk glanced down at his erection. "I just..." He sighed. "I just need to get on with it."

Sage smiled. "Yes. Exactly. And it will be better with practice." And he was so desperate to be touched he might stop breathing.

Kirk ran his finger's along Sage's length, then over his hip, drawing him close. For a few moments there was nothing weird, no doubts and no worries. Then he felt Kirk's hunger, his delight at being able to touch and kiss. The barren wasteland was seeing rain for the first time in decades and life was returning.

Sage's breath caught. He hadn't realized how lonely and empty Kirk's life had been. He poured his own lust into Kirk, wanting his mate to know how much he wanted him.

The kiss deepened and Sage kept one hand on Kirk's jaw while the other flipped the lid on the lube. Kirk tipped some onto Sage's fingers. Some slid through and landed on the floor, but he didn't give a damn as he stroked Kirk's dick.

Kirk groaned. "If you keep going that'll be it, and I know you want more."

Sage turned around and put his hands on the vanity. In the mirror he watched Kirk put more lube on his fingers then move closer. He knew the heartbeat before Kirk's hand touched his ass and traced the crack to his hole.

Kirk's caution and care almost broke him. He should've skipped the lube, gone for it and dealt with the sore ass tomorrow, but that might have scared Kirk off.

Sage met his gaze in the mirror. He couldn't wait any longer. "Please."

Kirk bit his lower lip, then nodded. The hot head of his cock pressed against Sage's ass, and then he was pushing in. Sage sucked in a breath, not sure if he was feeling his desire or Kirk's or if it even mattered when it felt so good tumbling through him.

Kirk sank a little deeper, moving slowly, inch by inch, his heart racing and his focus intense. Sage was about ready to come just from the look on Kirk's face in the mirror. No one had ever looked at him like that. And he'd never need to go searching again.

"Okay?"

"I will be when you start fucking me."

His witch finally complied. Sage clamped his teeth together to stay quiet as he met Kirk thrust for thrust, rocking back to take him deeper. His climax broke over him, hot and fast, almost like an unexpected shift. He groaned as he spurted on the vanity door. Kirk stilled and Sage drowned in his mate's delight. He shuddered as though coming again and dropped his head to his hands as he sucked in air.

Kirk's grip on Sage's hips lessened. "You ready for that shower now?"

Sage looked up. "Yeah."

He wasn't ready for Kirk to pull away, but they both needed a shower. And they needed to clean up the bathroom. But this wasn't a one-night stand. This was forever.

CHAPTER SIXTEEN

THE NEXT MORNING a silver electric car pulled up at the ranch. Almost every shifter on the ranch had decided after breakfast that today was a good day to pack a picnic for a walk in the hills, leaving only Sage's brothers, Mom, Violet, Ash, and Mica. They had felt the storm coming and now it had arrived.

A man got out of the car, looking like he'd stepped out of one of those fashion magazines from his styled hair to the tip of his pointed boots. The man stood there for a moment before his gaze landed on Sage, who was scrubbing blood out of the cab of his truck.

"Stone Madison?"

"Nope. Who are you?"

"Jude Sullivan, Coven Investigator."

"Stone's in the house. I'll get him."

But by the time he'd made his way over to the porch, Stone was already coming out the door. He greeted Jude like a friend he hadn't seen in a long time. "Good to finally meet in person. Though I wish the situation were better."

"I'd like to start by assessing the messed-up witch," Jude said.

"Kirk did nothing wrong. He was attacked." Sage wasn't going to let this witch—Jude had that feel about him—hurt Kirk.

Jude lifted his hands. "Never said he did. I'm only here to assess his magic and the damage that was done to him. I know you're his familiar. I get it; I have one myself."

That didn't make Sage trust him anymore. "I thought you were here for Mica."

"I thought I'd start with the easy problem."

Stone snorted and shook his head. "Good luck with that." He slapped Jude on the shoulder as he walked past. "You better take him in," he muttered to Sage as he picked up a clean cloth.

Sage nodded and put down the bloody rag. "Kirk's inside."

He opened the front door to let the witch in, then Jude blocked his way. "This is witch stuff." Jude shut the door, leaving Sage on the porch like he'd been a bad kitty.

———

KIRK PLACED his hands on the coffee table so Jude could inspect the scars. He'd seen the car pull up and had known immediately Jude was a witch; up close, there was something else. Like Jude drew his power from two different places. So, while Jude examined him, he examined Jude.

"You can just ask instead of poking around the edges. That's also considered quite rude amongst witches."

Kirk immediately pulled back. "I don't know any other witches."

"Your family?"

"Are dead. My mom...I think she was like me."

"She'd been corrupted?"

Kirk winced. "I don't know. But she sucked the life out of my dad, and I don't think it was deliberate."

"Honestly, any kind of witch can be turned into a vampire. It's a corruption of the energy magic we all use. It's banned magic, which is why your mentor was aware he'd be hunted down, much like the binding Mica did."

"If my mentor was already a witch, why do this?" He stared at his hands.

Jude paused before answering as though weighing his words "Your mentor was over two hundred years old. This is magic that is used to cheat death by stealing other's lives."

"My mom wasn't like that."

"No, your family were healing witches. But it's not hard for knowledge and training to be lost through separations, estrangements, or magic skipping a generation." Jude shrugged. "Healers naturally sense human energy. An untrained healer can be dangerous to themselves and others. Some give all of themselves away, wasting to death. Others automatically take what they need to survive."

"She never took from Abby and me."

"You were part of her so she couldn't."

Kirk frowned. "My magic was supposed to help people not hurt them?"

"We've all been there."

"You don't feed on people."

"I shut down a whole city by accident. Electricity is my drug of choice. I can't avoid it, so I have to manage it. Being a witch is like having a constant itch that needs to be scratched."

Kirk nodded. That was it exactly. Even if he didn't need to feed the temptation to brush against someone and have a taste was there.

"So, what do I do? Burn off the sigils again?"

"No. That would be really bad. I think you're managing your issue well. I've met nature witches who create more havoc than you."

"I'm not going to be hunted?"

Jude shook his head. "You didn't know. You were a kid, a victim. Unfortunately, vampires tend to take in those who are vulnerable and corrupt them, hoping to gather more to their side. There hasn't been a flock of vampires in quite a while."

"And the bond? I know it can be broken."

"It's gone way past that. You saved each other's lives." He held out his hand. "Can you do it so I can see what it feels like?"

"You aren't scared?"

"If you were going to attack me, one of us would be dead already." He smiled and Kirk felt the bear that was Jude's familiar.

He placed one finger to Jude's and took the tiniest piece of his life. Jude was like nothing Kirk had ever tasted, sharp and wild like a storm that couldn't be contained and at the center of it all was the strength of a bear, grounding him. Kirk pulled his hand back.

"Interesting," Jude said as though he'd just read something fascinating in the newspaper.

"What?"

"I just wanted to know what it was like to be fed on in case I ran into another vampire."

"Can I be fixed?"

Jude stared at him. "It's not a matter of fixing but unravelling—which is always harder. It took years to change you and it will take years to rework you. Do you want the training and the separation, or do you want to start your life here with your familiar and not worry about what you can and can't do?"

"I can do either, but not both?"

"I'll tell the Coven it can't be undone if that's what you want."

But it could be. He'd be a proper witch instead of a broken

one. He knew how to live as a vampire, though, not as a witch. And he didn't want to leave Sage and the ranch when he'd finally found a home where he was accepted.

Sage had told him to embrace what he was instead of running.

It was time to stop hiding. He was a vampire. And that was enough.

"I'll stay here."

"Thought you might." Jude place a business card on the table. "In case you ever need to talk to a witch."

Kirk picked up the card. There was a lightning bolt and Jude's name and number on it. "What will happen to Mica?"

Jude held his gaze. "He'll be given a choice, the same as you."

"What are his options?"

Jude was silent for a moment. "He killed as a cougar and not in self-defense. That's a serious crime. He bound witches which is just as bad. If you hadn't have stopped him, he'd have kept going until the human authorities got suspicious and that would've been worse."

"You're going to kill him."

"He can be stripped of his magic and his human memories and released into the wild. Or he can be killed."

"What do most choose?"

"Death."

———

SAGE SAT ON THE PORCH, waiting for Kirk to come out of the house. What was taking so long? There was no fear or pain though, so he figured Kirk wasn't getting hurt. He was sure he could find something to distract himself, but he couldn't force himself up. So, he waited.

Finally, the door swung open. Sage jumped up. "Are you okay?"

"Yeah." Kirk flexed his fingers, his knuckles cracking. His eyes were more orange than brown in the sunlight. "If I go away, they might be able to fix me."

Sage put his arm around Kirk and drew him close. If Kirk really wanted this, then he'd have to let him go. While they'd always have the bond, it wouldn't be the same as waking up next to him. Or starting a life with him. He swallowed the lump that formed at the idea of losing his witch so soon. "If that's what you want, then do it. Otherwise I'm okay with being a vampire's familiar." At first, he'd been unsure, but he wouldn't have it any other way.

Kirk relaxed. "I said no."

Sage sighed with relief. "Good, I don't want to let you go."

Stone came out of the barn where Mica was being held. "Why don't you take Kirk into the city to get his things? I'll do your chores for another week."

"Did Mom put you up to that?" Sage asked with a smile.

"Violet said Kirk might want to go and tidy up loose ends." Stone looked at Kirk. "You're moving in?"

"I guess so." Kirk glanced at Sage and added, "If you want me to."

"Yes, of course I do." How could Kirk have thought otherwise?

Stone took a step back and held up five fingers. "Five days."

"A week is seven days," Sage retorted.

"Don't make me regret this."

"Five days is plenty," Kirk called. "Thank you."

Stone waved it off.

"Shall we leave now?"

Usually Sage hated leaving the ranch, but after the last

couple of days, getting away had never been so appealing. "That sounds like a great idea."

Sage ducked his head and kissed the end of Kirk's nose.

———

Reviews are the online word of mouth and are greatly appreciated.

———

Don't miss the other books in the series:

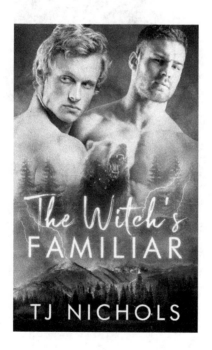

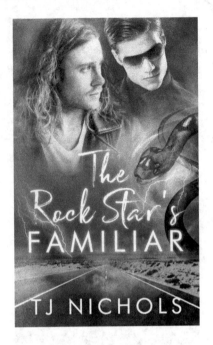

OTHER BOOKS BY TJ NICHOLS

Studies in Demonology trilogy
Warlock in Training
Rogue in the Making
Blood for the Spilling

Mytho series
Lust and other Drugs
Greed and other Dangers

Familiar Mates
The Witch's Familiar
The Vampire's Familiar
The Rock Star's Familiar
The Soldier's Familiar
The Vet's Christmas Familiar
The Siren's Familiar

Holiday novellas
Elf on the Beach
The Vampire's Dinner
Poison Marked
The Legend of Gentleman John
Silver and Solstice

A Summer of Smoke and Sin

A Wolf's Resistance

Olivier (an Order of the Black Knights novel)

Hood and the Highwaymen

Writing as Toby J Nichols

Ice Cave

ABOUT THE AUTHOR

Urban fantasy where the hero always gets his man

TJ Nichols is an avid runner and martial arts enthusiast who first started writing as child. Many years later while working as a civil designer, TJ decided to pick up a pen and start writing again. Having grown up reading thrillers and fantasy novels, it's no surprise that mixing danger and magic comes so easily. Writing urban fantasy allows TJ to bring magic to the every day. TJ is the author of the Studies in Demonology trilogy and the Mytho urban fantasy series.

TJ has gone from designing roads to building worlds and wouldn't have it any other way. After traveling all over the world TJ now lives in Perth, Western Australia.

TJ also writes action/horror as Toby J Nichols.

You can connect with TJ at:

Newsletter

Patreon

CPSIA information can be obtained
at www.ICGtesting.com
Printed in the USA
BVHW091149050122
625458BV00011B/386